The Strange Tale of Scruff McGruff

K.L. Miller

ISBN: 0615817815
ISBN-13: 9780615817811

DEDICATION

This is dedicated to those individuals and organizations battling not only Clinical Depression, but the stigma attached to it and other mental health issues. If you, Reader, think you surer from some form of mental health issue, I implore you: Seek Help IMMEDIATELY; don't allow stigma to destroy what God has given you. All Life is precious.

CONTENTS

ACKNOWLEDGMENTS

This book would not exist without the help of my editor, Katrina Walker, and a treasured Packmate Mrs. Melissa Morris. Both stood by me during the countless hours spent in excruciating agony as the words poured from my Soul. Thank you.

Dying Breath

By: D.A.M.

I inhale and

   taste Quiet Fear

FEAST

Instead...

   I gasp

   for Free Air

   Remembering its

   Flavors

Country Fresh and Pollen Yellow

Sprawl Stress/Gray Desperation

FREEDOM

INTRODUCING: THE DEMON CALLED MAN

Most Tales begin at the beginning. So I suppose I should start with my birth and go from there; there's a problem with that: I lived an unremarkable life.

I was born in the Projects and raised by a single mother and the extended Female Community she knew growing up. My biological father bailed the instant I showed my skin color; according to Family Lore, his mother thought I couldn't be his because my complexion was too dark. So... on her word he dumped my Mother, abandoning his First Born Child and Son; right here is where I guess many expect the start of a typical drug infested Life Story from Da Hood. I didn't go that route; between my mother, my grandmother and the other Females I found myself pushed towards something better.

Education is seen as the key to escaping a life wasted either drug dealing or hustling on the street corner; that's the road I was crammed down. I had enough natural intelligence to stay the course, but I also questioned damn near everything I was ever taught. And where others escaped life's dreary tendencies on the Streets I found art, writing and dorkin' out playing Dungeons and Dragons and other RPGs: anything capable of expanding my imagination and forcing me to think.

So... where did Demon come from, if **not** from the stereotypical cesspool known as the Inner City?

I am an only child; I didn't fit in with the hardened street toughs, yet wasn't genius-level smart. I did, however, fit in with the so-called misfits; even as a kid looking at thirteen as the beginning of The Teenage Years I hung out with what today is considered Goths, Nerds and other intelligent-yet-socially-awkward Youths. I began my love affair with technology in ordinary fashion: taking apart **everything** I could get my hands on; I remember studying circuit boards and wondering what the components did, how they did it and **why** they were needed. High School offered me the opportunity to delve into math and science, and unbeknownst at the time, gave me my love and affinity for writing.

Yet it was college that truly put me on my current path; I tried my hand at engineering, and like many students, took a job to help finance College Social Life: **Cooking.** I was good at it, and it seemed a logical choice; since I was single and had no foreseeable chance to *change* this, I'd better learn how to prepare my meals. This is where my passion for Kitchen Life seized control; it wasn't long before I looked forward to getting into the Kitchen, viewing classes as how I marked time between shifts. Besides... I enjoyed hanging out with cooks and servers; they seemed more Human than the engineering students and professors, all of whom found the constant number crunching Breath-and-Blood. Not me; I found pleasure in not only preparing meals, but knowing there were people who looked forward to certain dishes... dishes **I** prepared.

I earned my Social Stripes during those Kitchen Days and Nights. Yet it was in the Big Easy that I found what I'd been unconsciously searching for: **HOME**; roaming through the French Quarter, the Garden District, Mid City and the Upper Ninth Ward did more than give a small-town Southern Virginia Black Man a taste of Big City Life. Those years burned away childish notions, forging the hard heart and ruthless Honor I wield with Musashi-like skill and purpose.

I learned the cost of staying true to Who and What I Am back Home in New Orleans. I spent many long nights crying into my pillow, screaming questions at God. And yet I still managed to drag my ass out of bed to face yet another day; I taught myself to survive when no one wanted to lift a finger to offer aid or comfort. I learned how to love, and survive it being torn away; I wrote to ease the pain, sharpening my writing style and focusing my subject matter from explicit, gratuitous Smut Stories to character driven stories which **may** contain *erotic* elements. I was something different, and stronger than when I arrived; then... Hurricane Katrina.

I could easily put together a mini-novella about my experiences during this tragedy; I avoid it at all costs. There is little personal gain in reliving those days and nights and Horrors. All Humanity vanished; I watched Human Cruelty... and could not help but imagine what Hollywood would do with the truths. Yet I cannot deny the gaping wounds my experiences left upon my Soul.

My arrival back in Southern Virginia gave me more Reality than I care to remember. I remember attending church where I was baptized... only to have a big black female dressed in Sunday Fashionable *scream*, "You should get down on your knees and thank **GOD**; that was his judgment on that wicked place!!!" Two days later a Family friend wouldn't **stop** pressing for details; both were black females... and both looked at me as if they were expecting me to break down and grovel right there. I was an oddity... a new curiosity to be denigrated and slammed while they strutted around, **proud** of their superiority and status.

And there is the answer: Demon evolved from one Good Man struggling to hold true to himself and heal from tragedy while others in Southern Virginia, especially Black Females, did their damned level best to cram me into something socially acceptable for their twisted pleasure and amusement. Where surviving in the Big Easy felt like breaking free of some invisible prison, this feels like countless bodies hell-bent on clapping me in Normalcy's iron shackles. Things only worsened when I vehemently adhered to Who and What I Am, *refusing* to be restrained by local social restrictions and beliefs; never mind the

FOUNDATION owes its birth to those same restrictions and beliefs, I was Something Different. And different is the same as Hell-spawn to many in Southern Virginia; some things never change.

ON THE SHORES OF NORMAL INSANITY

I don't wonder about what anyone in the place will think about me; I'm a Black Man dressed casually and carrying a folder: **Job Hunter**. A few of the customers give me the standard eyes-narrowed-with-suspicion head-to-toe once-over before returning to their meals; one table seats four black females, all wearing what appear to be uniforms. I let my eyes drift around the dining room and discover their dress mirrors the two servers; I file the information away as I approach their table. The female closest to me turns right as I walk by, and from that movement on I know I'm being judged by a bunch of Bougie Bitches; fuckin'-A-**WONDERFUL!!!** So much for getting Good Vibes from this place; her gaze follows pattern: Face, shoes, attire... roll the eyes and display Royal Cunt Attitude as you dismiss him. The others snicker; I smile politely, choking down standard Dissed Nigga Street Reply, and move my gaze around as I search for a manager.

Gratefully, I manage to remove *FUCK YOU TOO YA GOLD-DIGGIN' HO* from my eyes before the manager pokes their head from the kitchen area; I'd have to *quickly* get used to such bullshit.

I wasn't at Home any longer.

* * * *

* * * *

I started writing when I was a kid. I'd work for hours on poems. Eventually I began writing fantasy short stories, but they never felt **good**; they always seemed to lack a true fantasy feel. While I did not completely abandon the genre I did set it aside for nearly a decade... while I worked on **SMUT**. The Polite Phrasing is *Graphic Erotica*, though I quickly figured out: **there is very little politeness where Smut/Porn is considered**. The cold truth about that genre: Humanity gets tossed aside in favor of dazzling, graphic details.

I also kept journals. Before the invention of online journal sites I used spiral notebooks when I wanted or needed to see my thoughts; it was because of my constant journal updates that I began wondering about something: character development. I was well into one smut story when I asked myself what motivated one of my characters sexually; then I asked this: what motivates *anyone* to engage in sexual activities. This lead me to stop work on that story and focus on how the characters got into their situation, *why* they decided to go through with it, what thoughts filled their minds during the act and most importantly, what happened afterwards? Eventually my stories shifted from graphic descriptions to thoughtful works filled with characters that were more Human than Porn Actor/Actress or sex addicts.

I honed my journal writing during my stay in the Big Easy; I also returned to the fantasy genre, and began dabbling in science-fiction. However it wasn't until I began a regiment of writing one short story-blurb every day that I can honestly say I tried to write something not only worth reading, but put together a longer, more complex storyline. During this time I found my descriptive styling wasn't... typical; heavily influenced by the Goth subculture and stereotypical African American Street Life, my stories reflected something I still have difficulty describing adequately.

After Hurricane Katrina my writing tended towards introspective journal entries and fictionalized accounts where I was the main character. It made character motivation easier; it also firmly established a darker edge within my stories. My physical descriptions of my fictional alter-egos strayed very little from my reality; though I do not have one specific dress style, my written descriptions revealed more than I knew.

* * * *

Where did THIS come from?

Good Question; the Answer... complicated. Doesn't matter; she can't keep her eyes from sliding over him... and he isn't her Type.

The black fedora looks odd on his head, even though the entire outfit **IS** Desmond Alexander Mathers: Scruff McGruff to his closest Friends. He always wears a goatee, and tends to keep a scruffy shadow-beard that varies in depth and darkness, though not always because of lax grooming or weather conditions. Small rounded-rectangular-yet-semi-Geekish glasses rest high on his nose; the lenses react to light levels, though there is always a soft brown haze lingering within them... **completely** invisible over his lighter-than-milk-chocolate-yet-darker-than-a-flavored-blunt-wrap colored flesh. Today's Gear includes a printed tee shirt: something new (he prefers the Layered Thug Look and **NO** logo on *any* clothing article). Around his neck is a hematite rosary; he was the first Black Male to wear one and many laughed quietly... until it became common knowledge that he came from New Orleans. This earned him instant O.G. status from many within the Street Life, status that only increased when the meaning behind *Black-Male-with-Rosary* became common Street Knowledge: *I'm trying to remember a few things about God... and it's too damned easy to forget. Once that happens I'll need His forgiveness.* The faded Levi carpenter's pants are held up by a belt and supported by semi-slender, gently rounded hips. Solid black boots complete Thug Image, though close examination of how the jeans hang on his hips betrays Layered Thug: there is some slack given, but not the around-the-middle-ass-crack-displaying-boxers Look demanded by Street Life. The Servers he hugs all remark about how good he smells: Cool Water, wine flavored Black & Mild cigarillo and fading marijuana funk hover above Fresh-and-Clean aroma. Then there is the black-gray-white flannel tied around his waist: part Skater/Grunge Style, imagining it on him is not only easy, but the overall image works in a strange way. And once the entire image is considered, it becomes frighteningly clear that his gaze never missed anything; as he is observed, so too does Desmond observe... watching the people who take even tacit notice of his presence and movements. The overall effect is, to some, between creepy and paranoia-influenced wariness; he always appears to be deep in Thought, even with his Pimp Stroll stride and lazy, polite Southern near-smile... and *not* happy Thoughts (as far as most people are concerned).

Adding a full smile on his lips does little to soften this image; quite the opposite. Occasionally speckled warmth dots his lips, but more often than not his smile lingers near The Joker's seemingly insane grin. His eyes are expressive, yet they tend to favor several disturbing images; it isn't uncommon to see them shift from narrowed, focused intensity to something beyond-ageless in wisdom, yet round and open and vastly intelligent. Yet those open Moments also bring something dark, alive only because it happens to exist within a human frame; savage, primal and barely restrained, hell-spawned Madness flares/flashes behind his glasses, illuminating already disturbing Features with cruel red and deranged white/sickly green/morning blue hues. And then there is the hellish Knowing stare that functions as The Normal, Day-to-Day Expression; his eyelids narrow and flutter-twitch, yet there is no focused intensity within the eyes. Instead there is only churning, chaotic darkness and infernal, emotionless Evil behind a gaze that, while physically unwavering, seemed to slither silently into their subject, seeing every shadow and prying into every carefully concealed corner of their Mind. Even when it brushed over someone his gaze seemed to sweep aside all Light and leave the Soul cold and naked. And there was never any trace of Humanity within that Knowing stare; only ruthless, emotionless Nothing looked at you: the eyes of Death's own automaton.

* * * *

Fiction writers exaggerate; this is a given. So it can be said that I exaggerate when I describe myself, but there's a problem with this; in order to exaggerate you must have *some* idea about the baseline concept. Since I am the baseline concept, what do my exaggerations say about me? One thing in particular: when I look at myself **I see Chaos and confusion and nothing Good**.

* * * *

* * * *

The bathroom needs cleaning, but I know the hostesses won't do it unless a manager gets on their asses about Doing Their Jobs; just another depressing thought, one I've shared with the therapist I visited. Yeah... African Americans, if you believe the standard hype, do not **need** therapists; they have alcohol, marijuana and reckless sex, better phrased thusly: *Drink ya sumthin'... Smoke ya sumthin'... **FUCK** ya sumthin'; this is how you avoid needing therapy.* And if you do not follow the prescribed remedy, what then? In general, the African American Community will say this: **go to church**; it will not say one word about the consequences, opting to point towards Religion as the catch-all savior for when you fall. However... one very real consequence is often suicide, one of **many** Silent Blemishes on the image of a proud African American; of course, according to standard thinking within the African American Community, *everything* outside of the Norm is considered crazy.

I'm not crazy; I just need to get the fuck outta this place. My Mindset and Code of Honor clash with Local Rules; I've worked and trained in Professional Kitchens in New Orleans. The kitchens here barely function, driven by egotistic Managers who tend to view anyone working in the Kitchen as their personal bitch or a criminal incapable of getting and holding a *real* job. I won't even go **into** my Dress Code: non-standard Gothic-inspired neo-Thug; I'm used to the stares and snickering, which means the seething, rabid rage I feel is less pronounced than when I first arrived in the area, emotionally dripping and ravaged by Hurricane Katrina's brutal destruction of my adopted Home. Unlike everyone in town I did not thrive on muzak and canned tunes; I need Music: Zydeco, Jazz, thundering Club Music, seductively ominous Goth rock and blistering Metal, sweetly flavored and smoothly blended World Music ... *CULTURE!!!!* It didn't take long for the Big Easy to win me over; everywhere I looked there was excitement and that pulsating Essence of Life Enjoyed. Variety is indeed the Spice of Life; as a Professional Cook, spices are something I tend to know very well; here variety's definition goes no further than one word: *different*, and different is **ALWAYS** Hell-spawned and blasphemous.

    I check my appearance in the bathroom mirror, slapping on a cock-sure smirk just for trial purposes; somewhere inside my gut there's a storm brewing. Probably Workplace Drama; spend **any** time in Culinary and you'll develop a sixth sense for what's happening in your Second Home: The Kitchen. I easily remember the fading memory of my chest covered by Chef's coat: *always* white; the smirk drips into a sad half-smile at the memory. Unfortunately I'm clad in Corp-grunt Casual: logo tee-shirt and black pants; I opt for cargo pants because of my love of pockets. Black slip-resistant boots, a fresh wax-and-shine, grace feet accustomed to boots; I glare at the baseball cap issued by the Corp and not for the first time... truly miss the white floppy I once wore with pride. Even with fresh-and-clean clothes I don't **feel** professional; I'm just another Trained Monkey as far as Management and the Corporation is concerned. I take a deep breath, swallowing the growing depression while focusing on surviving another grinding Shift. Career at a dead stop; and on top of that...

DAMN I need to Get Laid; no Ol' Lady, and just swinging my sick into random Silly Ho ain't my style (unless you factor in Skripper-Hoes; then again, that was always Biz... Never Personal). Problem here is: Sex equals *RELATIONSHIP*; and by Relationship I mean you'd better know for sure what role your happy ass plays in this: Back Door, Slippin' Bastard/Bitch, skeevy joker just out to fuck anything that'll hold still for a nano-tick. Hell... in this town being a Dirty ol' Man is **STANDARD STEREOTYPE!!!** Worse, he's got plenty of teenagers-wantin'-**ONLY**-Dirty ol' Man surrounding him; from there all ya gotta do is slide a bit to the left and right on the Kink Path to find your particular deviation. And if you *eliminate* sex from the equation and look **only** at friendship things do not get one tick better. By local definition: Friends are the ones who don't mind when you exploit and fuck 'em over constantly; **not** my Way.

My eyes trace the few gray hairs in my goatee, each one long and gnarled/curled/kinked-up; **more** and shorter versions dapple the close crop-top, though the are well away from the rapidly growing widow's peek hanging like a stone gargoyle over my annoyingly chimp-like features. Age and Stress from trying to stay afloat in a sea of depression cast curious shadows here and there, adding to the dark, near-Joker phantom-grin hovering over my lips...

dancing harlequin-care-free over my features. No Ol' Lady, and I won't do the Temporary - *Girlfriend*; I got over that bullshit when I stopped frequenting strip clubs. Having Side-Action is fuckin' **expected** for the males *and* females here. The entire area surrounding the city is ***THAT*** boring: Cheating provides gossip, entertainment and news if a body pops up (which re-ups the entertainment value as funerals are more Who-Showed-Up than mourn the dead). Fucked-up mentality from giddy-up, made worse because I'm known to be single.

Free Penis?!?! What's keeping the Ladies, **especially** the Sistas, from flirtin' with a Brotha... other than the moody nature and the whispered tales of me preferring White Females? Plenty; I don't react to Crab Attitude like other black males. I don't consider that shit attractive, playful or normal. I don't like hearing about my Home-Life from people I don't know. I'm a **very** private person and expect those in my life/existence to **respect** this privacy, *not* spread-the-word to everyone within earshot. I know that not *every* black female acts in this stereotypical fashion, but the majority here do; worse: those who do feel they are ***right*** to do so and will often cite the stereotypical Black Male as a source of their behavior. The African American Community has a Term for this: **GAME**; I don't play, one more reason I am considered a freak and spend my nights alone.

Then there's this: I am a Dom within the Lifestyle.

The Lifestyle: Bondage, Discipline, **SADO-MASOCHISM**; most won't go beyond the usual leather and whips. None know how it figures into the complicated formula representing Desmond Alexander Mathers; more than one believes anger is the source. Nowhere near the truth, but I'm used to that; stereotypes run rampant in Human logic. For example...

Broke Nigga ain't got the kind of cash it takes to build a dungeon in the middle of Da Hood, especially without someone finding out in a town where everyone is damn near *related!!!* And this is Hard Truth **regardless** of location: a Black Male in possession of **anything** related to BDSM (floggers, restraints, etc.) is OJ-meets-Rick James, Bitch! If I stick to racial stereotype, then I **am** allowed Rough Sex ala *every Rap Video/Song putrefying the airwaves* currently, but this eliminates my best asset: I have Imagination. I don't **need** a proper dungeon, just imagination and a near-psychic understanding of my **WILLING** partner.

That's what spooks most black females; its almost as if they can see me wanting to push beyond the Ghetto version of Spank Dat Azz and head straight for *Getting to Know You* territory, and all I've done in reality is walk by, smile a certain way as they Posture and Pose in whatever fashion they choose/prefer, and silently, RESPECTFULLY take in the sights. They check me out using Standard Black Female Procedure; I glance over them without pausing my movements: a Normal Human Reaction. Instead of Playa Spittin' Game I greet females with **MANNERS AND POLITENESS**; not sure, but I believe this screams *danger* to many Black Females. Danger... as in *he's a FREAK*; occasionally I get Uppity Bitch glare when I do this. It is a rare moment when I'm **given** polite manners. The black females I encountered in New Orleans were different, but only because they were used to polite manners coming from House Niggas, Hustlers running Game and black males working and living in fictionalized society.

I'm a natural at reading micro-emotions; so damned good it's one of the major reasons I'm single: hard to lie to me. And I cannot turn this ability off; believe me... **I've *TRIED!!!*** The Street Adage is this: *tryin' to Read me*, and I **do** read people. Every facial tick and Tell is known and processed. More... my skill is part natural ability and part Runnin'/Living in the Streets; years spent successfully dealing with Hustlers, Gold Diggers and every negative stereotype while adhering to a Code of Honor leave lessons that apply to many situations with few if any alterations. I've come to trust not only my instincts, but the end result of processing this constant Data Input; this leaves almost no room for surprises. So instead of constantly scrambling to keep up I appear several steps ahead; this is important if one is a Dom and utterly frustrating in so-called Normal Relationships.

Add those concepts together (instinctively and constantly reading micro-emotions, modern Rap/Media/African-American Societal takes on Sexual Relations and stereotypical Bondage imagery) and it won't surprise me if the casual observer blinks and shakes their head, confused by the sight and wondering, "What the...?" I won't be surprised if that same person looks at me with that same expression. Those who know me are so used to having that expression on their faces when dealing with **any** part of my life/existence that they start chuckling softly the instant the expression settles over their features; they know I'm not Normal, even if they don't understand the reason for my behavior.

* * * *

* * * *

It helps to define a word or phrase precisely; errors in translation cause everything from embarrassment to all-out war. This is especially true in relationships. While definitions clarify matters, they do **NOT** eliminate Drama; that requires Knowledge, Wisdom and Understanding. And those concepts are based upon time and patience, two things today's Society lacks. However, clarity has benefits, so I spend a great deal of time figuring out the definitions, making them solid things within my mind; the consequences of my attempts and any success: constant Social clashes.

* * * *

**Find someone who'll put up with your shit
and who's shit you can deal with: *THAT'S* the
one you marry and keep with you until the end.**
{{Big Easy Street saying}}

Ol' Lady. Ol' Man. They actually *talk* to each
other... fascinating concept; Alien Idea in Da Hood
here. But communication is ***NECESSARY*** if you, to
use the slang phrasing: do the Lady-in-the-Streets-
but-a-**FREAK**-in the-Bed Routine; with more and
more females *demanding* this treatment **and** the
understanding and caring ***required*** with it, one would
think communication would be vital to both party's
Mentalities. Check the rap music if you want the
answer to why this is not the case; the message is
clear, and counter-productive. Once you've crossed
over into Freak-Zone there is no return; a male isn't
supposed to love the Freak in his existence. Ever;
not sure which rule it is since I trashed my Rap
Codex as a kid. Keep your Freak away from House
and Home (these are separate concepts and
something which annoys me to no end);
House/Home is where you live, raise and care for
your family and Make Love (**only** Make Love) to your
Spouse.

I ain't got an Ol' Lady because I'm one dark,
twisted fucker; *shows* if you know where and how to
look or are psychic. I don't hide it because I'm aware
of the attempt: it pisses me off and I tend to explode,
the so-called Emo-Fit. So the Logic tends to follow
that if she has something similar occur, the two of us

wouldn't do well together. I would agree except for my Hard Wiring; I have an Ego, but it doesn't dip into narcissism.

If I see my Ol' Lady in *any* sort of trouble all thoughts go to dealing with her issues (see what I mean about dark and twisted?!?!?); I even have a Term for it, one the Streets and Da Hood are somewhat Familiar with: **Takin' Care of Home FIRST!!** Yeah... tack on those noble and honorable tags if you want; naked reality is this: if a Man wants *something* of stability within the four walls he pays good money to keep and keep up, he'd damn well better have this as Breath-and-Blood. Setting my shit aside for the sake of **US** comes naturally (**again**: dark and twisted); while I *hear* females cry for such a male, few know how to **relate** to such a male, probably because of scarcity of such males and no one showing them how to relate to one if/when they find him.

* * * *

Freak: the Word needs defining in each individual; internally and externally, it must be done if you insist on using the Term as a Label. Look Within and many see Spooky Places; looking at someone else: Porn; all well-and-good for this actually. Why? The 'off' switch on the technology playing the stuff and our ability to close the magazine; the Power of Free Will. Mind... it doesn't **delete** the material, and this fact must be fully understood.

Spooky thing: Free Will, because without it, you are not a Freak: you are *at best* **Property.** You become the oddity or Side Show someone visits when the mood strikes. You are put aside: a Tool used when necessary; and when a new and better Tool comes along, you *will* be replaced, and probably forgotten. Dehumanizing, yes; all too true, and done with depressing frequency.

With Free Will comes another matter of importance: **Trust**; it is **always** a matter of Trust. Physical safety is rather obvious; **EMOTIONALLY** you trust your partner even more. Depending on tone, *Freak* comes with either positive or negative connotations. Even facial expressions lend themselves to this; the negative connotations **will** leave emotional scars, and those damned things heal painfully slow.

* * * *

"So... you're big on defining things; how does that..." With her head cocked to one side and those doe-like eyes, one might think she's genuinely interested in my reply; I give the high-yellow heifer the benefit of the doubt because she's never encountered a Black Man like me.

"I asked when was the last time you had a lover *Play* with you; there are many different takes on that Term, but I refer to the Vanilla side of things.

"Which, sadly, is lacking in too many fuckin' relationships: the only time you touch each other is *to* Have Intercourse." I flick the ash from my wine-flavored Black & Mild, scowling faintly. "No passion, just Hit-and-Snore Sex; *BORING!!!*

"So. When was the last time you had someone take time and not just get you turned-on." I point at her heart, burning my gaze through that pulsating organ hidden behind Uniform and flesh. "Not **only** The Usual: whatever gets you off, but *then* do they take time to keep you stimulated. And I don't limit myself to strokes and continued fore-play: **can the joker make Polite Pillow-Talk if that's what it takes?**"

It isn't lost to me that I'm explaining this to a Gold Digger from the African American Community; I do good to ignore the snide look rippling across her face (*tear that Look off her face and devour the flesh!!!!*); I conceal my thoughts in cigarillo smoke, intentionally trapping a thick cloud between my glasses and eyes and forcing the scowl to deepen.. She narrows her eyes as she looks at my clothes (a bit useless: Work Gear makes us Drones); closer to my age, she's jaded and doesn't trust the words I've spoken or their tone. The nearby Twenty-Somethings and Barely Legals of *all* Racial Divides all turn their heads away; my words drip Romance, for damned good reasons, and they don't trust the darkness rumbling beneath the Romance.

The pale Goth Chic? Her eyes narrow; she hears the Ring of Truth... along with that ominous **something** that can only be Darkness. Funny thing is, there's a tall, BBW black female: MILF... and **she** hears that same something; I can tell because her gaze hits mine, then moves away, *dragged* by certain memories and thoughts. Though they are betrayed only briefly, she does check around once her Mask: *Big-Black-Bougie-Bitch*, is in place. Her gaze drifts my way once more; she's eager to see my reaction to the seductive pulse-twitch she gives her hips. I twitch my smile subtly, something **only** visible if you Know Darkness.

I know she's a single mother trying **not** to look like she'll be easy prey. Cougar on the Hunt perhaps; Looking for a Good Man **definitely**, and she's not alone tonight. Nor is she alone in wearing a Mask to cover up this Fact.

* * * *

Here is The List of Don'ts - African American Female Version: *I don't Suck Dick; I don't go near the asshole and don't go near mine. I don't do Kinky.*

Lies of course, but The List crops up fairly often; the revelation tends to chase it: come Go-Time a guy often finds himself eye's crossed and toes curled as she tries to suck his brains through his piss slit (already *got* the kidney). The only excuse for The

List: to maintain the respectable image of Lady in Public; close the doors and shutter the windows; **Freak!**

Now African American Males have a List as well, but it is complete bullshit. I prefer my Truth (one version of my words is commonly used when Black Males Spit Game at Da Club; easier to deny there because you're **drunk** after all, right?):

"Babygirl I got a stiff dick, nimble fingers, a wicked tongue and a *twisted* imagination: **WHAT'S OFF LIMITS???**"

And it doesn't surprise me when nearly every Female fixates on the Wicked Tongue; this is the Standard Heterosexual Male Lie: eating pussy is just like sucking dick. I'll take Gary's word for this: ain't no **WAY!!!** Yes Gary is gay; he tried eating pussy to *see* if the saying had any truth to it, so it ain't High-Horse Rhetoric from this sap. **SO...** when I see a black female eyeball me differently I know what to expect; this one doesn't disappoint.

"Most black men don't Eat Pussy," she sneers. I let Indoctrination settle on her face, meeting her arrogant gaze with a surprisingly cruel, dark smirk.

"I ain't *Most Men*, chica."

I keep my voice low and even, but it can't conceal my Dominant nature; nor does it do a damn thing for a favorite memory: being kicked off while Eatin' the Pussy. I'm *THAT DAMNED GOOD!!!* I remember the startled, wide-eyed amazement plastered to my partner's blue eyes as her brain tried to *function...*; I also remember the savage feelings and thoughts **at that Moment**. My eyes flash; the smirk threatens to sleaze into an evil grin.

"Well, I'd have to shave first," she replies.

"May I watch?" My voice is deep, arrogant, and completely devoid of Eager Geek; my words are nothing more than a question, yet there is cruel darkness in my tone, mirrored by the rapacious grin creeping onto my lips.

"**JUST** watch...?" As playful flirtation begins to brighten her eyes I shrug dismissively, the smile now fully evil, and utterly devoid of compassion.
Though... in Hood/Street Terms I'm just sizing her up, puffing on my Black, Posted Up in Pimp Stance.

"That depends on you." Don't do Kink; lie revealed. Most scumbags will hint at Anal Play here (if not outright ***ask...***), but I wait; her eyes say she is waiting for **me** to approach the subject... and I will... in a Way she is **also** looking for.

"Speaking of which: douche? Enema?"

"Why?"

There is silence; I smile; she hasn't *selected* one to Question; then again, she's Street-savvy.

She's also running on gossip and rumor: *Demon is a* **REAL** *Freak!!!*

"Douche is your Choice; I fully intend on sticking my tongue in your ass, along with fingers."

"No."

"Good day then." I turn and walk away, tipping my fedora as I do.

"Wait... just like that?"

"All or nothing, dear."

Silence; *I don't do Kinky... my ass.*

"You'd better..."

I raise my hand, stopping the tirade I know will follow. Got it covered, and in doing this my way I not only shatter the List-Lie, but unlock a door long covered in Darkness and hidden behind Normalcy. Not surprisingly, **I see Fear in her eyes.**

* * * *

High sex-drive and rough on my females; she likes that but can't carry body marks back home. She's single, so she does not have questions to answer there; her child will ask Mommy what happened and she'll be forced to lie. Yes it is cruel of me to have little empathy for her plight; I know too many Hood Rats who stroll in (to work **AND** Church) fresh from Da Club *stankin'* like sex, Newports, blunts and too much fuckin' alcohol. Even better, this ain't limited to African-Americans; Country Bars... Coffee Shops... the fuckin' Mall: same damn Mindset: **Lady in Public.**

However... her child is away for an entire week with Grand Parents; she needs the solo time more than she needs Sex, but the very thought of not having to explain why Mommy can't sit down right now holds decidedly twisted appeal. So she chooses her attire carefully, each piece designed to inflame Lust within my mind. Yet nothing suggests any derogatory Term; slacks accentuate her thighs, not skin-tight jeans requiring hours to wriggle inside. There is cleavage, not Tit Flash; makeup warms her features. The only Signs are those only a Player notices: no jewelry... not even earrings; if it can be lost and must be accounted for: no. Her hair comes from rush-job styling; this covers Freshly Fucked Hair if she encounters someone afterwards, and is easily excused with casually flippant dismissal beforehand. The final Sign: full arm coverage; the stylish fabric occludes any stray Passion Scratches without screaming their presence in defiance of the temperature of the night. Then there is the small purse carried in one hand: just large enough for travel items; perfect for the hair brush, Smart Phone and breath mints, it matches the entire outfit. One glance and Business Casual flashed across the Mind; she is quickly filed away among the countless others seen during the day, and easily forgotten.

As soon as she enters my place, secured behind locked doors and concealed by covered windows, she throws her tongue down my throat, groping hands eager to get things started; sloppy, until I take a large amount of hair in my hand and pull her away... just enough to growl:

"Blow me."

Command; she doesn't Comply immediately and there is good reason not to expect it here: **she hasn't been Trained**. This **is** what she wants, maybe **needs**, right here and now: rough, speedy Lust. I say maybe because she has a Love-Hate thing for sucking dick: so long as I do **not** place my hand on top of her head she's fine. Twirl hair into handlebars all damned day long and she's frosty; that one Sign of Ownership sets her off. Then again, many males consider her Strong Willed (read: **BITCH**); this Issue is just an example of that, if you subscribe to Stupid.

That word probably applies to her Former Lovers, **all** of whom had issues with Eating Pussy if one of her earlier rants is truth; too bad, since she tends for One-Up: Eat Pussy at all and she'll start toying with the balls. I had quite a blast discovering this out; now she benefits from knowing no Judgment for **liking** having a guys anus wrapped around her tongue. She still tries to bring me off **just** that way, but The Machine has some Mission-Specific Parameters: **stroke** the Dick if ye wanna approach, much less achieve, Orgasm.

* * * *

I think Strange Thoughts; this one ain't so strange, in my personal experience as well as Popular Media: Sperm Donor.

So. Would I, if asked by a close lesbian *whatever*, be the Sperm Donor for their child; in fucked-up Hood terms: Would I be Baby Daddy? And if ya stick to Hood Mentality, someone is gonna bring up **this** little shit-ball: will I be fuckin' her or is this a Chemistry Experiment. Hood Mentality: the Regression to Australopithecus.

Takes a shitload of time to come to my Conclusion: she's gonna have to prove to me that her decision is Solid with her Partner, within her **own** Soul... and *then* convince me; *CONVINCE ME THAT I AIN'T INVOLVED with that child SOMEHOW*; do that and I might consider going in all Smiles and Happy. Until then, fuckin' **pardon ME** for being a bit humbled and frightened; and if I look at you like I'm wondering when you got your day pass from Arkham asylum, you **EARNED** it. After all: *YOU'RE ASKING ME TO CONTINUE MY GENETIC LINEAGE... CONTINUE TO POLLUTE THE GENE POOL WITH DEMON DNA!!!* Then there's any and all Drama said situation brings.

Because Kali *asked* me, she's fairly sure I will not only say yes, but it is God-breathed *FACT* I and my Blood-Family will be involved with that child and she likes my Family; that's why Maggie, Kali's current Ol' Lady, is pissed at me. Maggie is a friend from *grade school*; we were lovers for a brief three months: Rebound Sex for both of us. Bad decision, and it was rough getting **back** to the decreased friendly intimacy when she goes back to her scumball ex and gets pregnant by his sorry, useless ass (**LONG** dull story); so I am not **HER baby's** Biological and this is where a piece of Street Experience comes into play.

Warning: that **ain't** Your Kid, but you'd better be ready for *her* to start lookin' to place the Title **Daddy** on any fucker who gets attached.

And Remember: I am **gonna** be attached. I love and care for and about both females; Honor and Duty guarantees this to be **FOUNDATION** for my relationship with *any* offspring: sue me. The only difficulty: defining **LIMITS**; and when Maggie's Baby Daddy makes a play for Kali and the *drama* pops off things may well force **me** to get involved, *and I do not have patience with Drama!!!!* Shit... I'm **guaranteed** one Drama Point: when he finds out about Kali being pregnant with my child, he's gonna **KNOW** she isn't pure lesbian and damn near **DEMAND** his shot. He is a true Single-Celled Organism; no higher or *lower* brain functions: instinct only.

Kali made her decision based on what she wanted and found passable; Maggie doesn't buy that, but I do: they have a great deal in common. Single Black Male looking for Lady-in-the-Streets-and-Freak-in-the-Bed-and-anywhere-else-quasi-

Legal... discrete, disease free, no Jail Time, working in a **career**...; that's me: Fresh Meat for Maggie and Perfect Candidate for Kali. I even got the whole Aged and Seasoned thing covered if that's what is required. Kali has an Oral Fixation (so does Maggie; I know **more** than a few such Ladies, thankfully!) and insists on her lover Going Down, one of the excuses Maggie's Baby Daddy used for bouncing on her (*really?!?!?*); Maggie being pregnant (with *his* kid now), he cops the Men-Don't-Do-Pregnant-**Ol' Lady** Hood Rule bullshit. Here's the sad, naked truth:

So long as it ain't **his** baby he's poking with his dick, he's perfectly *fine* with Pregnant **PUSSY. And he's a BIGGER jerk because I know another excuse** WHY **he avoids Maggie Sexually** (he uses Sex as a Pacifier: Maggie complains - stick dick in mouth to silence); problem is, he forgets: *ALL* Females are subject to Gettin' Horny. He also forgets this:

Stiff Dick, Wet Twat: NEITHER have a Conscience.

So. To the sick fuck wondering if I'm gonna have issues with my seed being knocked around by latex and silicone invaders, I say this: Mind your fuckin' Biz, chummer, and I'll do the same on this end. There are bigger issues involved.

* * * *

Here's something I've noticed: Freak stops where Normal Female ends. Not very profound, but try the example on for size:

Most females talk about Sex, but do **not** discuss Semen Disposal; Here There be Miss/Mrs./Ms. Freak.

Males are slightly different; you can bullshit about Spewin' Load here, there, everywhere, but in the end: **semen is meant to be Dumped, treated as trash...** not one-half of your legacy, Mankind, whatever, etc. Fuck... just check masturbatory synonyms and phrases: Toss **OFF,** Blow a Load**, and my personal *fav...***

Kill some Kids.

Never underestimate the depths of Human Depravity; as far as Normalcy goes, Sperm meets Egg inside Female: The End. All else falls under: Freak. Of course, Normalcy tends to skate over the in-between part of sex; Penis-sliding-in-and-out-of-vagina may sound clinical, but because we are Human... because we *THINK...* guaranteed someone will find this pleasurable, and thinking it pleasurable: that doth stray towards Freak Status.

So the question is: where is that Line between Normal and Freak; the answer may be found by taking a look Inside. Here I offer a warning: be careful when looking deeply within ones Soul for such things; those are dark corners **for a reason.**

CRIMES AGAINST THE UNHOLY

The only way to get to know anyone is to ask questions; of course there **is** one glaring loop-hole: you only know what you're told, and there is **no** guarantee you're given the truth or even facts. In New Orleans *actions* speak louder than words; this cesspool back-water is ass-opposite from Home, which means you get more liars (this includes **ALL** wagging gossip-tongues). Back home they go by another term: Mississippi Flotsam; here they keep breathing, continually spewing their filth, ***and spawning more just like 'em!!!*** There *is* a way to survive in such a place... survive someone turning the answers against you: tell the truth... with a smile on your face.

* * * *

* * * *

Virginian Voudoun Sunset

By: Desmond Mathers

"Where are you going?"

"The cemetery."

The Strange Tale of Scruff McGruff

I hear my grandmother's words; her tone spikes cautiously. My cousin doesn't look at me until I am well out the door... and I never look back to verify this. There is no need; I sense Fear from his bulky frame as I shift the walking stick from one hand to the other. I Feel his Thoughts drift towards his daughter... and those same Thoughts slot me as an Enemy.

This is my existence these days. Even though I am surrounded by Family, people *constantly* look at me with Fear burning brightly behind their eyes. They may mask it with a polite smile and forced humor/laughter but that is only for their benefit; I can See beyond their Lies. I was born and raised here; the Masks used are as familiar as breath and bread. I know the slight fluctuations in Tone that tell Lie from Truth. And I cannot forget the funk Fear leaves upon Human flesh.

Only in the cemetery do I find peace. No one comes here unless they have Business: putting someone into the ground and quietly forgetting their existence, if not their Memory. That is Tradition for many African Americans in my birth-town. So is the sickening tradition of going to funerals *just* to see who attends. As soon as I cross the threshold, casting a curious glance at the chain link fence, I Notice the difference.

I also take note of the caretaker; the building sits on the highest point. His attention brings a chuckle to my Thoughts; I Know the Why Behind. So does Papa Ghede; here there is only one Reason to enter a cemetery without a hearse: vandalism. I move along, picking up bits of trash here and there. The eyes follow me briefly before vanishing suddenly. I look towards the white building and catch the caretaker exiting the building; his eyes instantly snapping to my black clad, big stick wielding frame.

I picked up bits of trash and left-over weed-eater sting as I walked along the winding road. The Wind blew steadily, but I was only aware when I caught one of the many rude, brash voices on its invisible arms. I hear female and male, and catch a whiff of a blunt. I turn my head towards that Scent, knowing its location even before the winds shifts; eventually Physics catches up to the soothing dark Power that **is** breath, bread, and Blood-Right.

As I approach the caretaker I look at his face. White; he squints as he attempts to Read me for intent. I would laugh, but considering how many in this Town simply Assume, it is a welcome change. I ask if he has a trash can. He does, and in that instant I hear two things: age-slowed speech and the Years spent tending to the Dead. My presence bothered him; the care I showed confused him.

"Coming from New Orleans, you learn to Respect the Dead."

Another Instant... only this time I wasn't greeted by the shrinking thing suddenly bloated by Fear. Instead there is a different Equation displayed in his movements. Black Man plus dressed in black plus big stick... plus New Orleans equals someone who will respect the Dead. Anywhere else that same equations equals Voodoo. This is the start of the thrice-damned Bible Belt and Voodoo is not a Religion; it is Black Magic. In fact, anything that is not Southern Baptist is Black Magic, **including Catholicism**, so similar to Voudoun on many levels in *their* myopic view.

I continue on, taking notice of the simple things: Trees... Shadows dancing on tree trunks and along the needs-to-be-cut grass. Spring brings flowers, and already the stiff winds are stripping some from their new-found purchase. I reach a three-road crossroads and smile slightly as I Sense the absence of the

Fourth Road. The store to my left, a full half-block from my position, shows signs of Afternoon-Evening Life. I know that there is an outside trashcan and fully intend to use it.

I do not worry about the thuglings shooting the bull outside. The white wife beaters, over-sized tee shirts and overly sagging gear are nothing new. Their ages don't shock me; I have seen eight year olds with the look of a hardened criminal, **earned** by blood, not the Mask of a frightened child trying to survive. I have smoked with Snipers and Hardheads, whoodies and Goths, strippers, whores, drug dealers, pimps and other forms. Such experience shows in my stride.

Though there are a few eyes turned my way, none linger too long. They'll go inside and shoot their mouths off. They'll talk loudly about the strange black man dressed in black on a sunny afternoon... who carried a big stick as he walked from the cemetery. And they would laugh heartily until one of them asks the Right Question:

"Where's he from?"

"New Orleans," will be the answer, and the jokes will take a different hue. Light-skinned to dark they are all Black. And they will respond with Fear.

If you have seen the Harry Potter movies, or even read a book about the Arts Arcana, including **every Fantasy or Science Fiction Novel**... then you will know why. Mages with wands are deadly, if only because there is no telling what power comes from such a simple sliver of wood. For African Americans it is not the wand they fear... but the Ju-Ju or Mojo Stick.

For that is wielded by Houngans: Voudoun priests. Knowledge aids me here, and cripples others; Houngans have a counterpart: the Bokor or Sorcerer. However the mere *mention* of such an item wielded by a black man, and only one image comes into their drug addled brains: Zombies. From there imagination ventures into the dark realm of Nightmares and those stern warnings from old black women in tattered rags, rocking quietly back and forth as they Observe Life from their Porch or living room window... and who radiate Power.

I dump my second trash load and return. As I pass the store's front door I watch as a young black male, barely into his teens by the cast of his eyes, fingers a blunt-roach. His eyes snap towards mine and for an instant he wants to swell up with bravado. Something checks his attitude and he smoothly staggers to one side, slightly fumbling the roach. I nod; even those without Honor respect the status given by a Ju-Ju stick.

There is no Honor within the Streets... only Respect and Disrespect amongst those who claim it as Home. I find this sad, but not as saddening as the Fear I see masked quickly as I turn into the cemetery once more. Nor am I surprised that the crowd disperses rather quickly after I am well into the cemetery grounds. Those willing to walk amongst the dead are Unholy.

For there is still the Bible to contend with and according to it, I am a creature of Darkness and Evil. Why? Because I See both Realms, fear neither, and Walk as if I Know a powerful Truth. It is telling that should someone claim to have a root put on them they will not go to the Pastor with a Bible in his hands. They will seek out the eldest female sitting on the Deaconess Board: traditionally she holds to the Old Ways. Even within God's house such things breathe and exist.

Perhaps just as telling: the hypocrisy within the Black Church does not stop there; God is paid lip service; I frown as

this town's unofficial motto springs into my Thoughts:
Appearances Matter Most.

I stop at the incomplete Crossroads and cast another long
look at the Missing Road. There is Cold Truth to this; I smile
before finally leaving. As I make my way home I see the
caretaker leaving for the day. He salutes with one raised hand.
The speed and his gaze tell everything; not everyone fears the
Power that apparently radiated from my frame like Summer
Heat from blacktop. A drunken crack-head asks me to give him
the stick. For an instant I feel Anger ripple the calm surface
Thoughts... but only for an Instant. I know that if I speak
Truthfully I will soon be left alone... alone in a crowd of
Millions.

For the Locals will always Fear that which is not
Here/Now. Go to church on Sunday... and after the last amen
you can start gossiping about your neighbor, the one you just
hugged because the Pastor asked that you hug and love your
neighbor. Giving half is good enough, right? Come tomorrow I
will enter the Kitchen and once again be greeted by fearful stares
Masked by false friendliness and happiness at my arrival.

As I make my way home I ponder this. In every way I
defy the Norm here. From my ruthless, brutal honesty to my
Need to live within my take on the Lifestyle I do not fit here. I
do not walk, or talk, like a dumb, drug dealing Thug. I am not a
Black-Man/Redneck hybrid. In all aspects I am the most
abhorrent creature: ***AN INDIVIDUAL.***

Nowhere is this more apparent than in watching the two
Wicca at work. One wears her faith around her neck; I still
marvel at the inner strength it takes to wear a Pentacle in this
bastion of Church Mentality. I still recall the shift where I asked
if anyone greeted her in a proper Wiccan fashion: *Bright
Blessings*. I remember asking for permission to greet her

properly, and I remember the smile that tried to pull at her lips. Respect is not something she has known from the Locals. The other has always looked at me as if I was soiled and damaged goods unworthy of looking at her or her Ol' Lady. Yet on the Night when I spoke of my belief and respect for the Lwa, **all I saw was the same masked Fear I see day after day after night after night within Local Eyes**.

I do not wear my faith on the outside; it comes from within. So maybe the radiation that mutates their lie-based complacency into Fear is responsible for the Solitude I feel these Days and Nights. Maybe all I have to do is return to those crossroads and sell my soul... for Normalcy. The only problem is this: that is **not** a Deal Humanity ever wins.

Tomorrow will be another day. Maybe I'll pull out my copy of *Hagakure* and do some reading as I wait for Time to tick-tock by. Then again, studying such a Work will not help make me Normal. After all... it deals with Honor. And here, Honor does not exist outside of Uniformed Military and Police.

Definitely not within the Frame of a Black Man who dares claim New Orleans as Home.

* * * *

* * * *

"Have you *ever* dated a black girl before? I'm sorry... **WOMAN...**"

I snort, mulling over the memory as I swung the Black & Mild to the other side using my lips and tongue alone.

"Yes."

"That it? No details?"

"Why; are they important?" I dragon-spew smoke from the right side of my mouth, away from us; there's a brief, savage flash through my thoughts as I scowl into her face: *Tear her face off!!!*

"I'm being nosy." Shrug, Smile and Titty Bounce: incentive... and **completely wasted** on me. I have zero interest in her *sexually*; however, she may well serve a different purpose. I let my Joker's Grin spread swiftly, filling my eyes with mirthful madness, and quickly organize my thoughts.

"Ok. Run tell this..."

I like the nervous shudder she gives; it's the only time I find her even remotely sexually attractive.

* * * *

"Are you going to the Dance?" Well... at least she didn't complain about my last paper; still couldn't shake the Feeling that I'd missed something.

"No, Ma'am."

"Why not?"

"Don't have a Date; going to Prom Stag..." I shrugged; I **knew** I was missing something now.

"How about Elizabeth? Don't you like her?"

My Gut went haywire; I Heard a Trap spring inside the back of my skull: Classic Sign of being Hustled. Maybe it was because the Teacher was black and sponsored one of the pseudo-sorority of blacks, of which Elizabeth is a Member. Curse my Honesty: I answered in the affirmative. Next day, **EVERY BLACK FEMALE ASSOCIATED WITH HER AND-SLASH-OR THE SORORITY** gave me the same look: *When are you gonna ask?*

Bear strolled up and asked me about her at lunch, all but snitching out the Black Female Gossip Circle with ten-ton subtle hints, then Outing them completely:

"I heard you were gonna ask from ****; you know they talk, right?"

"The only one who knew I even **liked** her was Mrs. ****; what did she do... ask **for** me?" I remember flipping the fork and knife in my hand, wishing for a large black hooded cloak.

"Probably," he replied, stuffing a pizza slice into his mug.

"So I'm stuck." *Wonderful!!!* Blackmailed into this shit, and I walked **blindly** into it; SUCKER!!!

"Pretty much; go ahead and ask her."

* * * *

"Did you ask?" I smiled, hoping it covered the urge to rip her throat open because of the excitement dazzling her dark eyes.

"Fuckin' formality... and Death Sentence if I didn't; already had a few strikes against me. Nerdy, sci-fi goober black male; didn't hang with the *cool* brothas, opting for the Oddballs." My smile held more honesty now, driven by Thoughts of still cherished Friends.

"Your crew? What were they like?"

"My turn to ask questions: you don't like me... can barely stand to speak to me. Who blackmailed *your* happy ass into this?"

"No one!! **GOD** you're paranoid."

"And you're a liar; a **good** one, but still a liar; I know the answer already."

"Then why ask?" She spat her words, flashing sassy body movements that were *good...* but failing to cover the fear present in her shifting feet. Also: there was no real anger at being called a liar.

"Confirmation; killing two birds with one tac-nuke."

"You're an asshole."

She left with that, her attitude sharply defined in her Proper Posture; I didn't mind, since I got more from the encounter than she could possibly imagine. Not only did I know who sent her, but I also knew about her preparations before this impromptu meeting; no *accident*, she took the time to pry into my social movements before approaching me, choosing a location where she had ample witnesses...

Only one problem with her Back-Up Partners: one is a young black female who isn't really interested in my past stupidity; she's more interested in how I got into the Lifestyle. True to stereotypes, she figures it has something to do with one of my former **white** lovers; after all, **NO** black female enjoys 'that stuff...' But just in case there **was** a black female submissive in my past...

* * * *

* * * *

"Desmond? Can I ask you a personal Question?"

"Shoot."

"Have you ever been in love?"

"Yes."

"S... sorry; I didn't know..."

"Sorry? For what?"

"It sounds like you..."

Like I didn't care to remember the agony; observant for one so young. She lowered her eyes *respectfully*, giving me a chance to swallow the rising Emotions.

"If I offend you, I'm sorry. But... was she black?"

"Aside from family members, I can honestly say I've **never** been in love with a black female."

"Why not?" *There's* the indignant Black Bitch Attitude I've been expecting.

"Black Females are taught to avoid guys like me: Strangers. I don't dress like Stereotype-of-the-Moment; I don't spend my nights at Da Club, tryin' ta stick dick in anything that'll believe the rancid bullshit called Game. I prefer to treat Females with Respect, and without fail *EVERY* black female **HERE** sees *that* as a tell-tale mark of Bitch Nigga **they** get to fuck over and treat like shit.

"This town pretty much ruined me on Black Females."

"So... you never dated any blacks while you were in New Orleans then." I watched her think; fascinating... if painfully easy.

"Different; back Home I represent something between God-Miracle and fascinating oddity: Black Male with no Charges and no Kids. In New Orleans, that makes me the purest exception to the Rule; they're **used** to a guy havin' several Babies and Baby Mamas, not to mention runnin' from Fed Charges. If anything, I was a **DREAM** they've been conditioned to know as *only* a dream, never reality. And if I was real I dated White Girls; fucked up, and it didn't help that I **only** dated non-black females. Even the strippers I knew were mostly non-black."

"So you prefer..."

"I **insist** on a few things, one of which is Human Conversation. It doesn't matter about the Topic; I require an intelligent mind. Can't get that from a Hood Rat, Gold Digger or any other Female stereotype, race be damned. Don't give a shit about your horizontal Kung-Fu; can you stimulate and arouse my **mind...**"

Harsh, but better-than-Bible Truth; it just happens to be why I also stay well away from Drop-Dead-Gorgeous and avoid Hood Sexy/Miss Diva. I look into a Female's eyes, pierce whatever Wall she places as Soul Guard, and find the darkest corners of her Soul... the Places she hopes not even God sees; that's where *everyone* stores the Pieces of Soul inevitably responsible for so many misunderstandings and other problems: Plagues to solid Relationships.

* * * *

* * * *

"Dez; you ever fuck a pregnant woman?" I ignored his chuckle, focusing on **not** tearing his tongue from his mouth with my bare hands.

"You wanna know if I'd do Grace; before I answer, let me just say: you're a shit-for-brains fuckhead. And my answer... remains safely with me."

He tried coaxing it from me; I ignored him. Grace slid into the kitchen, silencing his bullshit for the foreseeable future.

If Grace wasn't white he would not ask; if she hadn't let on that she enjoys a **bit** of Kink in her sex-life he would not ask. He wasn't looking for What-If, he wanted details for gossip; not gonna give him shit, and I **know** he'll make up something to fit the void. I fully expect him to run to Grace, spewing lies into her ears; it **is** Standard Local Procedure when you wanna Start Some Shit, and he's *notorious* for it. Though... if he wants maximum Drama he'll wait until she's having an emotional Moment before springing his trap; he won't have to talk as much, meaning less likelihood of getting caught in a lie.

Game Recognizes Game.

* * * *

* * * *

"Desmond? Hey! Look... I was wondering... can we talk? I mean *outside* of work. Drinks maybe..."

"Nope, and I'll tell you why; Just Drinks means Sex is on the negotiation table. No disrespect to you, hun; I know the people around here all too well. Even if you suggest someplace no one here frequents you'll talk; it will come up somehow and you can bet the Stack on this: someone won't believe we **only** sat, drank and talked."

"I give you my word..." Her eyes flash brilliantly and she smiles brightly.

I stop her with a savage, low growl riding a quiet, hellish hiss; my face twists up as my lips reach for snarling. My eyes narrow dangerously and I lock gazes; my right arm vanishes from my senses, though I feel my right **hand** twitch as it rises suddenly. In the back of my mind I hear steel rattling within a sheath; blood pounds my ear drums... and I taste Death.

"Don't; I take such Oaths *seriously*; stripped of everything material, the only thing **anyone** has is their Word of Honor. I Follow a Code; breaking ones Word is unforgivable." She steps back, terror clamoring up her spine.

"So... how do you **meet** people? I mean..." She tries to avoid my gaze without appearing to look for an easy exit; I roll my shoulders and shuffle-step, twisting my head and neck, shoving the Demon into its Human-shaped lie once more.

"What you're looking for is simple: you want to know if I am an evil sack-o-shit 25-8; the answer to this riddle lies within Breakin' Bread." I force my breathing to slow, the deep inhalations silently slipping into the air. Blinking slow and deliberately, I break the spell holding her in place; I avoid looking at the usual Places (tits and legs in this instance) because Fear still grips her muscles.

"And that doesn't include going out for drinks; so... how does **anyone** get to know you?"

"Risk your Soul; Breakin' Bread means opening up that dark place within each of us and sharing. **TRUST**; if you cannot or will not Trust in the Seal of Solace..."

"What is that?"

"Best Street Phrasing: *Whatever happens or is said here, **STAYS HERE**.*"

"So... I'd have to meet you at your place?"

"Nope; anyplace we both feel Safe."

"Well... I don't know of anyplace **you'd** consider safe," she chuckles. "Don't think that's in anything I've read of yours."

"And that brings up another point: you Lurk; fairly sure you have your reasons. But it helps to reveal yourself; lurking in the Shadows only jacks-up the Paranoia level."

"I... **wait!!!** Write a story about me."

"Sure 'bout that?" I chuckle darkly.

"Yep; when you're finished I'll drop by and take a look at it."

"Why not email?" She has a funny way of pouting when shocked by something I say.

"So you **don't** wanna Break Bread with me?"

"Irrelevant; **what will you risk by coming by**; that's the real question, chica-love." Aside from the ridicule and snide comments, her answer would prove most enlightening; she stops the *I'm-cute* flirtations when she sees my face. Somewhere between apathetic evil and sadistic amusement, the near-sneer/grin accompanies a horrid, evil wildness glowing in my dark brown eyes; I wait for her to answer patiently... since I know what she will say.

CONNOISSEUR OF DARKER THINGS

Black, White, Asian, Hispanic, Mixed Race:
Irrelevant; *there's something about the way a
Female moves that just screams Dancer.* I don't
mean Stripper; they've **Danced**. You spot *Stripper*
in her eyes. Windows to the Soul is the phrase, but
focus on **Window** and things become even more
interesting, because who says Soul is the only thing
worth looking at? What about those Dark Corners
everyone has? And viewing the Soul **means** looking
at the end table holding up the stylish lamp; it means
the arrangement matters, perhaps even more than
the elegant emotional decorations.

And if she **was** a Stripper you can bet she has a
Monkey on her back; there is a truly Soul-corrupting
Pain within the Strip Club Scene, and drugs are not
the only Monkey. You'll find more than a few
Temporary Pain Sluts in the Industry, and more
screwed up Souls than you'll care to remember; the
reason is rather simple, if cruel: Cure Poison *with*
Poison. Meat Grinder is appropriate, and more often
than not... **the MILD Truth**; and those who Frequent
Strip Clubs find themselves quickly assimilated into
the Machine. That Old Fart who drops his
pension/monthly check at Da Club is One of Many,
Race and all other Barriers damned thrice. And
believe me: he's as Guilty of *keeping* the Gears
Grinding as he is of being Gear and Lube.

Why do they exist: Strip Clubs? Humanity; we **need** such places. Yep... some Females really **are** happy being Strippers their entire life; mathematics proves *that* much. Humanity functions on many things, and one of those happens to be the Knowledge tucked away in Dark Corners.

* * * *

Why **date** a Stripper?

Only two reasons; the rest are excuses.

ONE: Just to *say* you are dating/have dated a Stripper.

TWO: You want to have your girl come home and the first words out your maw be: "Bitch, where m'Money!"

And the rap lyrics are Cold Facts; sometimes she don't **wanna** Be Saved. Don't Play Superman, and be wary of Strippers pining away for someone to **don the red and blue** or some other Dream Romance with bling out the ass and Fairy Tale Happy Endings: Life is a Journey, and it ain't always easy.

* * * *

"Have you ever Dated a Stripper?"

"Technically, no." I let the exaggerated exclamations die down before calmly explaining... with a curious smile on my lips.

"Met them at Da Club; didn't make a move on them until they were out of the Grinder. Treated them like the Human Beings they were; that kept the Hard Core Hoes away."

"Why?" Female server; the cooks, *all Black Males*, paid attention. One lingered at his cutting board, the dish being prepared temporarily forgotten as he pretended to be lost in thought.

"Easy: Being Nice ate away at the Teflon armor they had to have just to drag ass into the place day after day, night..."

"Yeah... the Strip Clubs were **open** during the day in New Orleans; even on a Sunday?" Jo-Jo is an asshole; he also wants to keep his position as Resident Playa. His question is designed to portray me as just another sleazeball eager to fuck anything with two tits and a twat; I allow it, bending this my way.

"A few keep Blue Law Hours on Sunday."

"Man... all that young pussy..."

"Slow down, Jo-Jo; mornings you tended to get MILF Strippers, and don't be surprised if **GILF** is the best earner in the place."

"**GROSS!!!!!!!**" I face the speaker, features set in Kindly Older Street Gentleman.

"My dear Child, keep living; grow old enough to remember when your boyfriend went ape-shit nuts just *thinking* about Dancing Horizontal with you... and be confined in a body you'd **swear** belonged to your Grandmother... **not** on you." My smile: genuine; I know the truth behind my words. She doesn't like thinking about those days-to-come and straightens herself to her full height; it is doubtful **any** Female thinks overly long about them... until Tomorrow becomes Today.

"Ego; no Female living, dead or yet to be born doesn't **NEED** to be gazed upon with primal Desire. My observation... and damn near DNA; it probably won't go away with age... not unless the Female forces it."

"Church." I agree with the suddenly quiet cooks and servers: BUZZ Kill comment. I remain silent as Jo-Jo's smart mouth fires off something I instantly block out. In this area, Church is seen as The Answer; that may be for some. It doesn't take away from my words or their cold, naked truth.

* * * *

Stiff Dick and Wet Twat; neither have a Conscience. God really doesn't enter the equation **during** Sex unless you count the fact that, for Believers, Sex is **PART** of His Unknowable Plan. Before and After? This is where debate happens; Children and Parenting factor here: **Responsibilities...**

And Choice; **FREE WILL: GOD'S GREATEST GIFT.** So... I chose to Enter and Leave that Life; learned quite a bit, and have scars and nightmares from Hard Lessons. And don't start in on choosing ones Sexual Alignment; just another Choice, based on what one likes: **the Reason we do EVERYTHING...** including Going to Church. Unconscious thought is **still** thought, and it helps to **THINK** about Sex before you do it. Less Trouble and Drama...

* * * *

I like giving and getting hugs; gotta **like** the chica first however.

So when a new server runs her hands along my lower back as she glides by, the incidental and *necessary* contact triggers my Alarms, yet I find myself surprised by **HOW** she touches me... and Snarling Angry Black Man pulls up short, the *snarl* actually hesitates, like something wasn't quite right for true Anger to manifest. **So** surprised that I vividly recall her image even now... and the fact is I was flashing back to a Strip Club:

She was a server back then; yep: some clubs in the Big Sleazy served **food!!!** Or they have waitresses bringing you drinks; New Server and the images from my past fit perfectly because of how new server moved her hips. And this wasn't the first time I'd seen her; Small Town Hood and she rode the bus with me on many weekends. Struck up something of a conversation and got a clue about her past, but I was too busy basking in the *refreshing* conversation with a Black Female!!

So when several other black servers start up, and **Stripper** comes up, Jo-Jo asks if New Server used to be a Stripper, but she doesn't answer.

I ask, "Say... you used to Dance?"

"She used to be a Stripper," a server chimes in.

"Didn't *ask* that or you. Hun... you Danced; it shows in the way you move." I appreciate the Female Body, and Dancers, **all** Dancers, swing their hips with this swish/**pop.** New Server *answered* me, but it was the silent Thank-You dancing warmly behind her eyes and soft smile that completely crushed Angry Black Man.

Later, Jo-Jo says, "Dez... you won't surprised..." He *starts* to smile...

"Nope; know **too** many Dancers and Strippers from back Home to *not* notice the body's movements. A good server has similar moves; learns 'em ducking and dodging everyone from BeBe's Kids to Drunk Fucker at the bar."

"Gonna get dat Number?"

"Why you in my Biz, yo?"

Had damn near this exact same conversation in more than one Strip Club back Home... and **every**

Kitchen I've ever worked in; just hoped I didn't have to cut Jo-Jo's tongue out of his mouth for being a smart-ass. It didn't help that the fajita steak was **shaped** like a human tongue; I wondered how his would taste, flavored with the shit he constantly spewed.

"'CUZ!!! And you were just bull shittin' about some Gran'ma Strippin'..." I sighed, *carefully* setting the eight inch Chef's knife on the cutting board before speaking.

"She put her daughter through **LAW** School; owns her Home, and **OWNS land**. All from Workin' on the Pole; Hustle Money, ya 'eard me? Don't think they *only* earn and put that shit up the nose; Death come quick dat way, ya 'eard me?" I forced my voice to remain even, yet black/green Rage and disdain still colored my tone.

"Daughters takin' care of Family; Single Mom raising a CHILD... keeping Roof over heads, clothes... Life; stop using Labels and look at the **WOMAN**. Few *enjoy* Sex-for Money; it leaves Scars that won't heal completely. Ever."

"You loved her..." New Server; I smile, and would **kill** for a cigarillo... and neon darkness, music loud and ignored as I Inhale the Image before me: Stripper and Server... Labels I peel away.

"Nah; she was someone I knew from the Strip, hun. **Gotta respect the Game... and those who Play well.**"

Sometimes Beneath ain't pretty; but I've grown rather fond of watching Single Mother struggling to Feed Child and Tend to Family any way possible; though I am dismayed by how *few* Men are at their sides or within their lives... all too few. Plenty of Scum; lots of Closet Freaks and Fake Friends as well. Look to the SOUL within the frame; dangerous, but every now and again I catch sight of something truly beautiful.

Sex is Business in the Strip Clubs, and in more than one Normal Business/Industry; internal Cold is necessary. It isn't justification... just a damnable NEED if she wants to see a Brighter Tomorrow. In this she is Normal, and it bothers people who *think* they **are** the Norm because *she* sucks and fucks for her money while they don't. Hey... if you wanna be ruthless, I know plenty of House Wives who **exist** solely because Daddy makes the Cash and they cough up Ass; same Shit, different Toilet: Deal.

And she just might go to bed alone, tucking in Child and **still** worried about Unseen, Unknown Dangers; **LOVE** doesn't care that she is a Stripper, and a Mother's Love knows no bounds... Fears no Danger... *right?* Bartender... Server... Stripper; that Child Knows only MOM, and I will back her if she is PROUD of this Responsibility; Instinct on my part... and the only Right Thing to do according to my Code.

There may be Tears; she may loath her Life...
Monkey or no-go Mojo, it doesn't make a difference:
She is a Single Mom, and it Hurts to Sleep Alone.
Pain. Necessary Lies... keeping that Child in the
Dark... struggling to escape to someplace better;
sounds Normal to me.

* * * *

With regards to Sex, **Hop-In-Hop-Out** can't be
done without Scars; think otherwise and enjoy your
horrific Fate: you earned it, stupid. Doesn't mean
thinking your way around the Scars ensures minimal
Pain, either; it only means you've ***chosen*** how much
you'll hurt, bleed, and hurt again. Remember that;
it's an important, hard-earned Lesson/Wisdom.

I find it difficult to divorce Race from the Lifestyle,
and I won't *blame* Tradition/Teachings and History. I
will say this: Never Underestimate the Depths of
Human Depravity, or the lengths Mankind will go
through to justify ***anything***. Put as I was taught in
those Moments-that-never-happened: only **Rich**
White Folk did such things; ask me, it felt good to
bore my eyes into a Female and see something melt
away as *submissive* crept into her Soul, if not **from** it.

Ask Tradition, Black Females...

Yeah... get a **BIG** hush there; so I'll Speak what
I've experienced. She may long for it, so long as she
gets to Church, Plays the Role: penance-face,
Holier-than-thou or some other bullshit; you can

keep Side Action Dick for your Freak Pleasure, so long as Home is Secure and Daddy don't find out or don't mind 'cause he's doin' the same damn Dirt.

Then again, from the Black Perspective: MILF is **always** Blonde White Female; dark haired White Females: Cougars or Raven-Haired Vixens. And if you can't shake stockings and dresses from the image, congratulations: you, like me, are part of the Brainwashed Masses. This image is Normal; try slapping it over **any** Black Female, and one thing happens that I'm not sure is all me: **Classic BBW**: Female with Curves. Why? Healthy-equals-Curves is the traditional Excuse/Reason dredged up; if not this, then *Affluent*, and even **then** you don't expect rail-thin to grace the Mind's Eye. Food... *and the Money to Eat Good*; somehow this, to me, smacks of internal Racism/Stereotyping.

Stripping Race from the Lifestyle Equation is difficult for me because I **am** conditioned to Think: **no** Black Female can find Pleasure or enjoyment within the twisted Pleasure and Pain found there; though if I think about it, R&B Songs are packed with Strong Women who stick by no-good Males because those Males are Good to them in all ways except Wandering. Emotional Pain is *still* pain; funny thing is, I figured out part of **WHY** the guy Wanders: you ain't supposed to Get Freaky with the Wife/Ol' Lady. You trust her, but *never* with the Darker Side of Who You Are. In short, Shit/Trash gets Dealt With *outside* of Home. Always. Sounds noble... and to me, is about as ass-backwards as shit gets.

To be honest, writing stories about Black MILF having Dark Thoughts intrigues me; raised by a Single Mom, only now can I honestly admit: everything I got came from her and her boyfriend, the Man who raised me. But if you believe in Follow the Stereotypical Bullshit, I'm supposed to write Afro-Centric Tales featuring Mothers like Claire Huxtable; sorry... don't know any. Know a shitload of Tara's though...

Tara got pregnant before she was prepared; you can fake-and-fudge relativity on that point, I won't, sticking to **her OWN** judgment and words. She had the Child, kept the Child, and Deals with Shit. She still feels the pull of Da Club Life, bright lights and plenty of Eye Candy/Bling... Good Times, at a Cost; Tara goes through Baby Daddy Drama, might even be the Nightmare Baby Mama to this schlub, but that doesn't really matter: the Shit still stinks and must be disposed of, preferably **outside** of House-and-Home. And in the middle of all of this, Tara still enjoys Sex; she may have some views that clash with the Norm, but hey... she's Makin' Due with on-hand Materials... **same as everyone else.**

With Tara and many like her, Race can be erased *quickly* with another color: Green... as in Money Green; from there, just look up and down the Money Scale; you'll find Tara everywhere: Rich Bitch on the Hill... Trailer Park... struggling to Make

Due in Da Hood; no other Divide seems to matter once you focus on Money. Tara is the sexy MILF behind the bank window, **the server** you can't keep your gaze from because of *those tits*; there might just be a few Females sipping on their double-shot caramel mocha, doing everything they can to keep from **being** Tara. Maybe she's the Female you scream at for driving with her Smart Phone glued to her ear while driving with kids piled in the back seat; stroll through Wal-Mart, Target, Macy's or any other shopping center (*especially* Malls) and gaze around: there she is... guaranteed.

Tara: just your Average Female; she Wants... she Needs. So I'm not surprised to find Tara attractive; not stunned to see submissive Tara-Slut behind the Proper Social Mask demanded by judgmental Souls stuck in Stereotype-be-God-Truth. Tara is a normal, healthy Woman.

And Tara is a Pain Slut; pregnant again, her sexual encounters leave a void within her, something she couldn't put her finger on until she happened upon a Dom and stuck her head Down the Rabbit Hole. In this case: clothespins on her always sensitive breasts. To be clear: she enjoys Rough Sex; what she endures was, and wasn't, Rough Sex; indeed, she sneers at considering it **Sex** at all, though she is afraid of the reason why:

Emotions; no matter what anyone thinks or assumes, Pain touches Emotions. Having a dick slide in and out vagina is Status-Quo Pleasure from another Soul - **The Norm**. Pain... *from the same Soul* - only in Domestic Disputes if you adhere to Normal Standards; once they mix, the Human Mind finds it difficult to undo the end result, a mashed concoction that is as bizarre as it is, **to me**, fascinating. For Tara, as with many like her, there is that Dark Tone within their Thoughts, ominous and dangerously Hungry; it manifests as one simple word, though the power behind it cannot be confined therein: **MORE.**

However, Tara must Exist within Polite Society; so she keeps her Freak carefully concealed, masked by jokes and chuckled comments or buried beneath dogma and-slash-or Religious teachings/traditions. **ALWAYS KEPT WITHIN THE DARKEST OF SHADOWS, THOUGH...** and this so happens to leave tell-tale Marks; it affects every move they make, and I see and notice them Instinctively. So, to me, Tara really is the librarian; she is that nurse with the wide hips and natural smile you remember. Tara is the MILF you spied during Open House, eyes bright and ever sharp despite work, chasing down her rambunctious kid and dealing with teachers and spirits knows who else during the course of the day. And occasionally Tara loses control; anger spills from her mouth and rattles her body. And more times than she dares recall, Tara cries.

She is every Woman; she has Needs, Wants, Desires, and occasionally, they are very Dark indeed. **She is all too Human.**

* * * *

When Bethany, a server, was pregnant, all I *heard* from the other cooks was about how sweet and wet Pregnant Pussy is; not one fuck-head happened to mention the curious connection that **is a Factor**: the Unborn Child. Emotionally as well as biologically attached to Birth Mother, not one cook bothered to take the Child into consideration until the jokes about poking it in the head start up: Brain Damage... probably explains them more than they'd care to admit. And when I asked about Long-Dickin' their whatevers during Pregnancy, ***universal answer: NO!!!***

Why? Started getting frowns and screw-faces, like the thought of Sex with their girlfriend/Ol' Lady **now** is abhorrent: Testosterone-based 180 Before-and-After. Stupid; worse, they won't stop fucking during those nine months, so they pick up Side Action Pussy. And **this** is considered Normal; personally, there isn't a Term for this kind of egotistical stupidity.

"Oh... so you'd be tyin' her up and shit **while** she's pregnant?"

"If that is what she requires, yes." My answer is smooth, yet there is nothing cold about my Tone; I speak from experience. ***Terrifies*** them however, though I'm not sure if it was the words, **OR THE HONESTY IN MY TONE**; probably both.

* * * *

The Child is connected to the Mother, and right now, every inch of Mom wants to be *Fucked*; pull-the-hair, tap-dat-azz Mandingo Gorilla Grunge Fuck. So... on our next visit to the Doc I bring up the subject. Why?

I flopped in The Big Easy; if there's one thing I understand about its Citizens: they **will** be True to Who and What They Are; if that means she is a Pain Slut sexually, with the sensibilities of Middle-Class America, then I expect more than one Doctor has been questioned about Rough Sex as well as Bondage during pregnancy. So Doc's cool, professional reply was not only a blessing, but proved one thing: Mankind goes through great lengths to have its cake and eat it too.

So... Pulling Hair, Restraints, Forced Lactation... these and more lay tucked within my memory; Dark Skills, Safety... Instinct now, so they are beyond the snide comments from over-eager dweebs. And when it comes to light that someone I'm actually *cool* with is pregnant, I understand and know the barrage of bullshit Cook's Humor about to fly my way. Doesn't matter how I meet it, so long as I get mad *according to Local Standards* so that everyone can laugh and gossip about things they know nothing about. Play it cool and level-headed and *somehow* I'm her Back Door when Daddy can't or won't scratch that particular, peculiar dark itch.

No one considers her a Human Being at this point; not one thought is spared to the Child unless accompanied by crude, vile humor. And I am **supposed** to Fiend for Pregnant Pussy, consider someone I care about as Temporary Pussy (with the Option to keep it going if my Game is that Good, yo).

"You need a Freak, yo."

"No... just one Good Woman will do nicely, thank you." I smile, returning to my work; it helps cover the thrice-damned, unholy chuckle rumbling through my Thoughts. It doesn't keep raw evil from the corners of my eyes, so I focus on my work.

* * * *

* * * *

Work Flow Interlude

By: Desmond Mathers

Time for another Work Week; Fresh-and-Clean, got Tunes pounding the walls while I dry off, and an Ol' Lady quietly drowning out **my** bass with the mournful Gothic Music she favors. I am not ignoring her and she is not unaware of my presence: this is Biz.

Time to get into Cook's Mode; gonna be a busy Weekend and the Kitchen isn't the place to be thinking with your genitals... during the Rush that is. Afterwards is another story, and in this case it means she gets more than her fair share of Sex. If I'm right, Mother Nature will show up in a few days; maybe I'll wait...

Besides: she likes the Show; putting myself into Kitchen Mindset means finding an internal Groove and riding it all the way through the shift. Today it's Tech N9ne; perfecting my amateur Spitfire Staccato (styled after the Tech N9ne's Midwest Chopper rapid-fire lyrical delivery) may be just Pipe-Dream, but when I hit a Rhyme Cypher with some of the Dish Crew I like to at least *try* **to** bring SOME Skillz to the Arena. Of course... she likes Strange Music (Tech N9ne's Entertainment Machine), and when I Feel her standing behind me I can't help but smile. She moves Between my Thoughts; I Love her and she understands me so well.

I really miss those Big Sleazy Days and Nights.

Now it's just Tunes and Ghosts; I puff on my wine flavored Black & Mild quietly as the day's tone shifts; I let the music flow while imagining the entire restaurant, Guests included, trying to Feel its Energy and Flow. I try to remember every local event I've caught a glimpse of during a commercial or haphazard glimpse at the paper; I process every slip of Data about the After-Work Social Schedule the town keeps, then forget it. It's known... and I'm ready for it. Slowly, a deep chill settles over my Thoughts; it spreads to my arms and I stretch my neck, frowning slightly as it cricks/clicks/snaps/pops. For several agonizing moments both shoulders freeze up, pain splitting my Thoughts deliciously as I adjust my stretch to relieve them.

"Getting Old Blows," I exhale/growl, smiling as endorphins and Delta-9 flood my senses; can't be helped though, and if I do say so myself, I've done better than expected. Actually I'm rather **proud** of the gray hairs and sore, work-stressed bones and muscles; means I survived a few scrapes, and still have miles to go, energy to spare... and a nagging drive to keep Moving Forward.

The room is a mess, but I look and smell Fresh-and-Clean; worn boots shine with a fresh coat of wax and muscle-sweat; the Layered Thug Look works well for the encroaching Winter chill, with the Black-and-Gray-and-White color scheme adding to the dark, brooding Look I've cultivated. I scoop up my MP3 player and smart phone and saddle-up for the bus ride: no car and **bad** Recession in this small town means hardships; nothing new, but when you feel Million Dollar Big and ride the bus: Ego Bust. If I had an Ego; been poor most of my Life: Familiar Turf, just like Hard Work ain't no Stranger. Got nothing to prove to a damn Soul, just myself; a Kiss Before Dying (one more Hit) and I'm off into Normalcy once more. Another day in Paradise: Big Easy saying about heading into the Workplace.

Then there is the Promise to keep to God: Bring Honor to The Streets, even if it meant Standing and Dying Alone. I'd *like* an Ol' Lady... Kids... all that crap, but not at the Cost of Honor; it'll be worthless... less than that, and my Worth beyond nothing.

"And they won't understand." I chuckle darkly, amused by the truth even as it saddens me.

So. I'll make them understand.

Puff twice, this time from Jakar the Dream Killer, the small green and black glass bowl I smuggled from Los Angeles a few years back: vibe before Go-Time...

And into the Night, damn the sunlight; it's running away anyhow. You can say its just going through the usual routine; I say: it can't stand the Creatures of the Night today's society demands.

* * * *

* * * *

"Most guys run from a woman raggin'; you don't." She eyes me, waiting for the Dark Thing everyone calls **Demon** to emerge. I stand beneath the lone security light, though not directly beneath it; the large cardboard receptacle shields me, and the tree limbs over the brick wall allow Night's darkness to seep into my own shadow. Were it not for my cigarillo's soft cherry-glow the eye simply places my motionless form as part of the natural darkness: *Feels Good and Proper.*

"Nope; just a Natural Process. The *real* danger comes from the mood swings; gotta keep on ya toes then."

Menstruation, Pregnancy: Natural Process; any hang-ups come from the mind; it helps to get over *fast*, since they aren't changing any time soon, damn scientific efforts. I Feel my Thoughts stretch out, grab the darkness and pull it tighter around me; only natural after I fired off that rancid Standard Guy Response about mood swings.

"You ever eat a girl out while she was on?"

"No; more than one Female, and a few Women: no Girls."

"Pardon me..." she smiles right as a cramp hits; the mixture of emotions on her features is interesting, and I imagine the Scent filling her panties... ***thong if memory serves me correctly.*** I ponder the sneer pulling at my lips, sliding my gaze towards her eyes when they narrowed slightly. I remove my smoke from my lips, cloaking my face in gray/blue/black shadow.

"Yes I have my Red Wings, dear." I let smoke pillow up beneath my glasses; great excuse to screw-face, covering that part of me that wants to drag the conversation into her Trap **specifically** to destroy it, preferably with great fanfare and cruel, demonic glee etched on hideously deformed yet grotesquely beautiful features. I flex my Right Hand as images of her terrified expression flash through blackened storm clouds; when I finally inhale, the fresh air tastes foul. I flick the ashes onto the ground, darting my gaze to the sudden faint light as the cherry reacts to excess oxygen.

She's got an Ol' Man; she's just lookin' for Side Action fun, and *everyone* wants to know something about Demon - the Super Freak. The worst ones are the under-age hostesses; mostly working nights and weekends, they get the bullshit tales and lies from Gossip Tongues. The only good thing about that: I don't have to rip off their pretty young heads because of mistakes; I'm allowed to show compassion. Downside: they flaunt those Illegal Bodies while *checking* to see if you're looking, eager to add another experience to their surprisingly (or not) sexual encounters. Doesn't help that I always look into their eyes; they **bounce** titty, and when I don't drool like an idiot: Fear flashes behind their eyes: yes, dearie, *I AM THAT MEAN, CRUEL, RUTHLESS AND HEARTLESS.* Now go ply your Tricks on one of the other Males around; or Females: I know more than one server here *eager* for a lesbian fling with some Young Flesh. As for the Female looking to make me her Back Door: Been There... Run That... Too Rough... Pave it.

* * * *

I could look into her face all day and night; getting lost in her voice is a Blessing. So plastering Pimp over my features *should* be difficult.

It isn't; my expression is no Mask: **Pimp cometh from Within**. Yes I Love her, but right now: m'Money ain't lookin' right. This makes Daddy *very* unhappy; look at me wrong... breath funny... and I'm liable to slap ya silly. And so long as m'Money ain't Right, I'll *try* to look at her fondly, and **that** is it; can't spare Love. My Heart aches because of it, but until m'Money is Right, she's gotta make due with the emotionless shit pile I offer. Even hugs lack complete Humanity; they feel rushed, devoid of true warmth.

So why hug at all? Same reason I wear my Rosary: to Remember; there **is** something Good in that simple Touch, and I *should* be looking for it and indeed, I need it in my Relationships and Life... but ***m'Money***. I can't think straight... can't be Human... until that's Solid and Lookin' Good. So... Pimp; I smile and look into her eyes, dredging up as much Human concern and compassion as I can while I try to ignore the bills piling up *just* because I know the fridge is running, keeping what little food I have fresh and viable. I listen to her while mentally swearing at the Sixty Cycle Hum I sense, a **constant** reminder: m'Money ain't Right.

* * * *

Minus the downsides: having a Monkey on your Back, feeling humiliated, used, etc., here's why Females have Stripper Fantasies: **they like being Looked at... Admired/Desired from afar**; the whole Money thing... you'll get Excuses and disturbingly gentle smiles. Every fully-functioning Male, and more than most of those who are not-so-functional, ***enjoys*** watching attractive Females Bump-and-Grind to Music. Don't be surprised when you notice a few **Females** in the mix; I've seen more than one MILF *accidentally* step into a Strip Club, eyes locked on some svelte dancer doing her best to make the chromed pole lose a load just like the drooling males transfixed in their seats.

Now here's where shit gets muddled: if you follow the Stripper Fantasy to its Darkest Conclusion, you get Sex in the Champagne Room: Down and Dirty, **with NO Emotional Attachment afterwards**; this is where shit breaks down as far as Fantasy within Relationship goes. This is coming from a guy who spent **many** hours in dark Strip Clubs: when a Guy **KNOWS** it is Temporary Pussy, he **will** treat you like shit in the end; the Polite Ones spare you an honest smile, but they leave **everything** there in the dark, stank corners of Da Club, chica-love. *NO WOMAN ENJOYS BEING TREATED LIKE THIS, AND MOST WON'T STAND FOR IT*; in a Relationship that shit will be the Death of Love.

So how is the Guy in the Relationship *supposed* to Act?

LIKE THAT IS HIS STRIPPER!!!!

Property; so don't be surprised when *that* Look hits his eyes.

Treads heavily on Pimp Thought, **and there hasn't even BEEN Sexual Contact...** just the THOUGHT of it: basic Logic Flow of How Shit Shakes Down. So I'm not surprised to find MILFY who *demands* this as her Ending: Daddy takes the Stripper Home... forever; for more than one Stripper this is Fantasy. For some, the Reality mutates into Sugar-Daddy; this is where Terminology tries sweetening the Lie: she's a Ho and he's the Client.

Trust me: it's a **GOOD** thing to know where Fantasy ends and Reality begins.

* * * * *

I won't Date a Female *unless* she is bisexual; that said, I do **not** give a shit about Sexual Preference where **FRIENDSHIP** is concerned... except for Lesbians (**LONG** story...).

First: I don't give a shit who anyone sleeps with; I have Twisted Views based on my experiences with People in general. What **you** do in the privacy of *your HOME/House* is your business... **NOT MINE OR ANYONE ELSE!!!**

Second: because People are involved, the Basic Rules don't change: Never underestimate the depravity you'll encounter; Biz... **never** Personal; Money First, everything else is Second best at best. These are Standard Rules of Sexual Encounters in today's Society.

See... Guys Talk Shit about their Techniques and Skillz, and Females do also; Sexual Preference doesn't alter this fact at all. So **if** you can talk about it intelligently, compassionately and with humor, cool; if not, I'll still smile... just lament the loss of a potential Friend. I've got a shitload of **those** in my Wake; one more is the Norm so long as I keep living. You can't really separate Preference from the Soul; you **can** choose to not Target Fixate on this or that. I find that keeping a Wide Stance tends to be best. It's how I've found my strange cavalcade: Those I Call Friend; a strange and motley collection, and I Love them all, smiling at their Memory. Individuals, one and all:

PEOPLE; I don't think Testosterone Monkey, fag, gay or dyke; those are Slams, not Terms of Endearment.

If there is Conflict, it comes when outside fuckers start making assumptions; been through the whole *you-gonna-try-and-Turn-her-from-the-Dark-Side* bullshit with a few lesbian Friends, and got into a fight with a guy with **TWO** bodies on him already because of it. Earned serious Street Cred that Night because I stayed True to my Code: don't fuck with my Friends; Mind yo Biz. I got no Fear of Death and don't care How I Die. That is Street Love from a Hard Heart, nigga. If I call her My Sister, you'd better *believe* she is **that** close to my Heart and Thoughts; don't jump to conclusions, and do **NOT** think for me. If you ain't hear it from these lips it ain't Bible Truth; believe that.

BATTLE SCARS ON THE SOUL

I. Need. Pain.

Once I had an Ol' Lady who liked to bite and leave marks; I told her there was only one Place where I would allow her to indulge herself... for the moment. I miss her and the connection we shared.

There are Times when Pain is the only thing capable of shattering the overpowering clamor inside my head; I Need something to snap me back into here and now, **while** satisfying that thing inside of me. It feels like a funky Logic Circuit; get both and suddenly I'm back in control. And that thing, the Demon, can fade ominously back into my dark, blemished Soul.

I. *Need*. **PAIN**. Too much Normalcy... too much Status Quo; I long for that primal white-hot sensation: beyond Passion and thousands of Realities beyond sexual excitement. **PAIN**.

Guess even Demons get Battle Shakes...

Ancient Proverb: *Be careful what you wish for.*

* * * *

Prologue

76

From: Journey of the Damned - My Personal Journal

Now I sit back and think of what I've done... looking beyond my personal Code of Honor; those Thoughts will tumble through my Mind, perhaps making their way into The Teachings or another philosophical work languishing among the other incomplete stories. I've Busted a Home to Get Mine. I've seduced a Trusted Friend. Not to mention that you're a Co-Worker... and Here/Now, the only Soul I Trust there... and the only Soul who dared try to get to know me *outside* of the Kitchen. And for my transgression I receive Pain... enough to swallow a legion of damned Souls.

* * * *

Hurricane Katrina.

Nothing more need be said really; she destroyed many lives. I don't dwell on property damage or anything materialistic; those things rely on Money. In the Big Easy, Hustler Mentality is breath-and-blood; even the well-to-do understand *and* abide by this natural tenet. I landed back where my Blood-Family's roots are deep: Southern Virginia; I didn't want to return there because I **knew** that Place and the People there would do whatever it took to kill me. I was different and different must be eliminated at all costs in my birth town.

For example: the first Sunday in the area I attended church where I was baptized; I guess I was searching for warm Christian company in a familiar setting. Maybe I was hoping to Feel God's presence.

I was also plagued by gnawing memories of just how shady and duplicitous some of the members were; childhood memories of After the Sermon gossip sessions still roam my mind and while I hoped things had improved, I wasn't holding my breath. The older members know my family and they greeted me with restrained smiles... especially the males with a Military background. Yet it was the *FEMALES* who turned paranoid Thought into cruel reality; I wasn't someone fresh from a traumatic event in search of God's Light, *I WAS SOMONE WHO'D BEEN THERE AND* they *WANTED EVERY SICKENING, GORY DETAIL. RIGHT FUCKIN' NOW!!!!* I managed to semi-smile my way through them until this one Big Black Heifer jabbed her finger at my sternum and in her **LOUDEST** Bougie Bible Thumper high-and-might voice said these words:

"YOU NEED TO GET DOWN ON YOUR KNEES THANK *GOD* FOR YOUR LIFE; THAT WAS HIS JUDGMENT ON THAT WICKED PLACE!!!!!"

She looked at me, self-righteous and **proud** of her Words; I'm not sure what she **expected** to see from me. Probably wasn't the sadistic Rage that filled every nook and cranny within me, or the quickly donned Mask I threw over it; I honestly believe God steered me away from her and **pushed** me outside of His building. I'd lost trusted friends in that nightmare; I know Mothers frantic for information about their scattered Family members. And this cunt had the *audacity* to **DEMAND** I turn my back on them?!?!

Yeah... **GOD** save her that Sunday afternoon; He saved her from being torn apart, her organs thrown into the street after I ripped her throat out right then and there.

Go home.

Not in the Big Easy; all I can do is head to my flop and get sloppy drunk. NEED to get High but don't have the Connections.

So. Find a Kitchen; if there's one thing I've learned about the Service Industry: Kitchens *always* have at least ONE Weed Man on the payroll.

Never set foot in that church after that; not unless my grandmother asked.

* * * *

Back in the Big Easy I was, within the African American Community, something different. No kids. No charges. Thirty-plus years old; something *had* to be wrong with me. The Reality: I learned from Southern Virginia - *never* get caught Doin' Dirt; it didn't matter what the Hustle was, **have no less than three escape routes ready to go at the drop of a hat!!!** Also: don't **look** like you're up to no damn good; Appearances Matter is the First Law within my birth town..

Roaming Canal Street, Mid City, the Marigny-Bywater, the Garden District or the fabled French Quarter *without* looking like Standard Thug was dangerous; looking like a **LOCAL** meant I got fewer looks. My eventual dress code blended Goth with Street Sense; if the Image doesn't fit in your mind I can only say you've **never** hung out around the bottom of Decatur Street, where the Gothic sub-culture flourished: another Flower blooming in the French Quarter.

Black Females in New Orleans didn't know how to approach me; when I greeted them with cautious respect and nearly instinctive politeness I received suspicion and frowns tainted by Street hardness. Over time it became apparent: I prefer quiet honesty and respect to the loud Crab Attitude; after a few incidents I earned Street Cred **and** Respect. Eventually one Female approached me. I will not say she was timid; she wasn't **used** to Being Nice first. When her actions got her kindness and honest respect along with admiration I saw something I'd **never** glimpsed within the Black Females in Southern Virginia: hopeful self-confidence and Pride. I will always remember her as a strong, dedicated **Woman** and Mother; she helped alter my decidedly negative outlook on dating Black Females.

Back in Southern Virginia, that outlook came roaring back with the force of those waters spilling through the broken levees. I saw **too** many Females stuck portraying negative stereotypes and *proud* of their classifications; I saw too many slamming those they considered beneath them while steadfastly doing the things they just berated another for doing.

Duplicity seemed natural... a Birthright; worse, they expected **me** to respond in stereotypical Black Male fashion: they - crab attitude... me - attracted and playfully Street Aggressive, the so-called **Swagger** mentality.

I'd just lost everything I'd worked to get. I'd lost close Friends and seen my adopted Home nearly obliterated... its Citizens abandoned without a first or second thought. I rested my head knowing nightmare memories from three days and nights within the seething cauldron that was the New Orleans Superdome; the **last** thing I needed was some stuck-up cunt belittling Who and What I Was. I could not forget the lessons and **would not** forget the bright Souls, the true Thugs struggling to accept the Trap that was Big Easy Hood Mentality and those hell-bent on building something *BETTER*; something within me screamed: *Tell the Tale no one wants to hear.*

I was alone in a crowd of millions once more; it wasn't where I **needed** to be and there were many Nights where Suicide seemed the better alternative. I wanted to return Home and asked many to help me, including Managers at work and Social Workers; none offered more than lip service. Behind my back I caught whispered slams and cruel jibes and slams; each word drove me closer and closer to self-destruction. Each broken promise tore at my sense of Honesty and Honor until the only thing left was a hellish monstrosity barely confined and controlled by decades of adherence to a personal Code. I didn't even have religion, just Faith in God... and **HE** seemed set on *allowing* this torment.

So I wrote; before and after every shift I sat before an aging computer monitor and put my Thoughts down. Fueled by nicotine, caffeine, THC, sugar and alcohol (but *only* at night; Never Drink before Work - Personal Rule) I poured my Thoughts and Soul out; within scattered stories and ranting, rambling journal entries I regurgitated my constant battles with depression and the nightmare assaults because of my Social solitude. I'd spend hours burping out dark erotica and science fiction, painting vaguely beautiful and incessantly dreary, overly paranoid images complete with Male protagonists fueled by their personal Code of Ethics and utterly confused by their random, bumbling Quests for Love. It wasn't long before there was less-than-nothing Human within my Mind and Body; whatever remained of my Soul lay tattered and covered with rancid filth. Desperate for relief from what felt like thrashing in ever-changing, oozing, storm-tossed seas stocked with Flesh-and-Soul eating parasites, I begged God: *give me ONE Soul who'll make the effort to Understand me... someone I can Love without fear.*

Lesson from the Big Easy: **be careful what you ask for; *you'll get it AND A SHITLOAD MORE!!!!*** Especially from God; He gave me Amy... and with this *gift* came a near-fatal blow to the last dredges of Humanity within me.

* * * *

It began with those tits; the instant they popped into view I was distracted... and focused on their owner, my favorite server. She moves with ease and confidence and simple grace; it is painfully easy to Work with such a wonderfully beautiful Soul... especially when they are damn good at their job.

I controlled the music, selecting tunes best suited for everyone while **not** offending anyone; the Line ran Liquid Cool, enjoying the musical stress relief. Only Expo remained as any weakness... until Amy took the Position. There was a smile on her face and I Knew the Why Behind. There are multiple reasons, most of which deal directly with my presence. I'd bellowed earlier... something that guarantees management will be twitchy. When they asked what was going on I told them: find me an Expo I can trust; so... Amy.

Enter my favorite server and those amazing, always distracting tits. Her smile brightened up the Line considerably, and my mood quickly shifted. A Proper Cook and good Expo combination is a true wonder to behold; yet I must admit... I never lost the Master's Tone with Amy or anyone else. And I made it a point to look her in the eye and thank her for her assistance. *Say what you Mean; Mean what you say.* She smiled and her perfect Gothic tan reddened sweetly; I could almost Scent its sweet, seductive aroma.

Now it must be said that I danced and sang while on the Line, things I am known **NOT** to do. Aside from adding a light Mood to the sheep, it gave my favorite server a chance to see me when I'm being a fool on the Line: a very rare happening. And I didn't check her reaction... just danced. Full Big Easy Cook-Mode; nothing Mattered but putting out good, safe, quality Food in a timely manner... EOF. The end of the Shift simply appeared; one minute every cook was bangin' out plates and the next: End Game. Stations got cleaned and prepped for tomorrow; jokes bantered about while plans were made for the Night and beyond. As usual, my plans included a fresh bowl-pack and single malt; I let my gaze wander over the bodies still present, unsurprised by the absence of my favorite server. However, Amy remained, her gaze squarely on my face; I smiled.

And... she faded without a parting word as all Expos are want to do.

Even so, when I needed a strong presence Amy was there and did her Job; it never occurred to me to question why. This would prove to be my first mistake.

* * * *

Broken Glass

Let me Lie to you for a Moment:

Straight from Katrina, my Mindset was Survival; one chica (not Amy) made the effort to be a Friend, but I questioned her motives. Why? This is South Central Virginia: The Genteel South and start of the Bible Belt; no one *ever* makes Friends unless they are looking for something to exploit or burn up. As far as Local Tradition was concerned I was New Penis and single, aka: Prey. **True Predators have Survived Being Prey**; sure I needed to Get Laid, but I have a Rule:

Get to Know me before ya end up with my Dick in yo' mouth; this means talking **to** me, not at me and most **DEFINITELY** not *down* to me; right there... problems. Not sure about the details behind the *reasoning*, but Local Females have a nasty habit of treating anything with a penis like complete shit. Not that the Males are much better; being an unfaithful, lying scumball is normal here. Unfortunately this *Get to Know me* attitude means, at least as far as Locals are concerned, that I am looking to Settle Down; not the entire Truth, but Locals here avoid even *thinking* about the Truth since it **is** poison in the veins and more Soul destroying than a $300-a-day cocaine habit. She took my attitude at face-value and in the process our friendship solidified; sounds like a Happy Ending, so what happened? Local (some would say societal, and I would not argue against their position) bullshit:

So I'm forced to secret away any Opposite Sex Friendship, and this makes me feel like someone's Dirty Little Secret; odd thing about that is, most Females here *assume* that Males **don't** have Feelings, thus they cannot feel as I do. If a Male does possess feelings, he's weak: a world-class Puss-Ass. According to Tradition, the only excuse for a Male and Female being friends is SEX; I've actually lost a Friend because of telling her this: "Let's just be Friends." Apparently that means *I don't want Sex with you and therefore, have no need/use for your company.* Her reaction is, to be polite, fucked up; it fairly guarantees she can't cope with other Relationship Issues, such as talking to one another, being **open and honest**, and most importantly: **TRUST**!!!

I prefer to base my relationships on **Friendship**, foolishly believing Friendships are *based* on Trust; if I don't wanna stick dick her then, according to Local Tradition (utter rank ***BULLSHIT***), **I'm the one with something wrong**. I should be fucking everything willing to bed a nigga or drunk enough to hold still for a second; I need to smile at titties in my face and allow the Sexual Flirtations that border on harassment room to fester. But genuine Respect and **COMPASSION**; these concepts are forbidden in an inter-gender friendship.

Now... this Woman is popular, and has many work-friends including a few Males; one, a **MANAGER,** runs his mouth in certain Gossip Circles;

it seems he didn't approve of the Friendship I developed with her. What was the Gossip? Remember: they are Friends, apparently for some time; so imagine my response when he said this: *He ain't **REDNECK** enough for her!!!* And WHY would he say such a thing about a FRIEND? He and a co-worker were swapping lies about who was fucking whom. Yep: Friends are **only** for Fuckin' in that shit-hole, and I'm talking about the **town** as well as the Restaurant in question; doesn't speak well about how he sees her, but hey... if I listen to Gossip: *I was a threat to his chosen Side-Action Pussy: HER!!* No need to listen to it; **his Ol' Lady/Wife** got wind of his cheating and made several late-night appearances, *always* timed perfectly: when he planned on sending everyone except his Side Action/**GOOD FRIEND** home and, because he's a **MANAGER**, CRACK OPEN THE LIQUOR AND GET HIS DICK WET!! Guess Wifey wasn't completely dazzled foolish by his new income increase. All of this Drama... **because a black Male made Friends with a white Female**; and this is the truly sad part: she was the **only** person within that Kitchen who dared reach out to me, the Soul still tormented by Hurricane Katrina's devastation.

It's bad enough that I'm struggling to overcome Hurricane Katrina's devastation; I also have shit like that lurking around every beautiful smile and warm, friendly greeting.

* * * *

Love and Hate within the Damned

"What was the worst Kitchen you worked in, Desmond?" Before answering I stop cutting the scallions

"Corporate Bullshit: Casual Family Dining. Also known as Gourmet Fast Food..."

Cooks within Casual Family Dining are considered the Necessary Evil and treated as such. They may be someone with seniority, but the cook wields **NO** authority; Cooks, even ones with years of experience and company loyalty, are there to cook the Food *ONLY.* Corp Kitchens *assume* all Cooks have zero interest in making the Kitchen a career; cooking is a means to Legal Paper/Legit Money, *not* a Career Choice. In the Corp World, **Career** means you want to make insane dollar amounts and sit in an office; Career means you despise physical labor. Cooking isn't considered a Career; there's no Upward Mobility within their view of the Kitchen... just empty Pipe Dreams of being a television Cook/Celebrity.

I couldn't convince Amy otherwise; she wanted me to settle into Management. **Stick** with the Restaurant Business... just leave the Kitchen; she never understood what she was asking me to do: **THROW AWAY MY DREAMS AND NEARLY TWENTY YEARS OF BLOOD, SWEAT AND TOO MANY TEARS!!!** Though she never said it, I'm certain this was one major contributor to her Silent

Treatment: I wouldn't blindly Chase Money and adhered to my dream of being an Executive Chef.

Yes I am intelligent; I chose my Career. I love my chosen Profession dearly; it is part Art and part Science. In my twenty plus years I've come to see Food as something more than Chow... something to make a turd; I've come to know my Customers as more than an Income Source. The Restaurant isn't just a way to make money; it serves a need within the Community. And my thoughts are **not** childish Ideals; done properly a Restaurant is something *everyone* sees as **PART** of the Community, not just one more leech bleeding them of their hard-earned Money.

* * * *

I started cooking in college, but cut my Culinary teeth in Private Fine Dining; that means there was **one** Owner to deal with. I got ultra lucky: the Owner *loves* the Industry and their Place; they treat Employees as **Family...**

A Kitchen without Leadership is destined to fail. I've worked in a few Kitchens and know this to be hard Truth; the Kitchens most likely to reveal this: Corp Kitchens. I've learned to select Kitchens with strong Leadership; typically this means there are both a Chef and a Sous Chef: **professionals** dedicated to the Culinary Arts. Without fail, **NO** Corp Kitchen has anything beyond Kitchen **Manager**; Managers are driven by Numbers. They think *Labor*

Costs and *Bottom Line*; they are taught to **deal** with Human Factors. Customers are Income Sources and are manipulated with that concept foremost in their minds.

Hurricane Katrina took everything from me except my life; I ended up in a Corp Kitchen just to put food in the mouth and keep a roof over my head. I **asked** them to help me with the one thing I knew I truly needed: **a way back to the Big Sleazy**; guess I counted on Virginia Hearts having more compassion. Shows how mind-fucked I was; before we parted ways I left a trail of searing terror and nagging nightmares within co-workers and Management, not to mention being pushed **over** Depression's jagged edge.

*You don't Summon Demon unless you **NEED** shit done; he'll get it done... regardless of who he's gotta kill, mutilate or violate.* Had to teach *everyone* there this Truth; New Cook meant sucker to everyone, *especially* the Females. Pushed and mentally screwed, I stepped outside to Pray as Papa Ghede guided, and **that** meant a salt circle and blood. When dealing with Demons, whipping out God tends to start wars and carnage; I knew it would frighten everyone, and the instant Management tried to hold my job over my head in order to get me to **stop** praying when I got pissed, I pulled the Intelligence Card: Religious Freedom. I forgot: **no one** likes an intelligent Black Man willing to fight for his Rights... ***ESPECIALLY IN THE SOUTH!!!!***

I'm a practicing Voudoun; they're actually **fortunate** I don't bring out a live chicken for sacrifice. Dance with a serpent and I *might* get a few strange looks (there's a sect of Christians who practice snake handling). Learned more than the Name and Face of the Demons tormenting my Soul; the Kitchen actually has one Poltergeist as well as an Ancient: an entity so old it *appears* demonic. When a server commented that one of the morning Prep Cooks said the place was haunted by a Ghost I corrected them; the Poltergeist does not like being mistaken for a Ghost, and **really** gets upset in the presence of duplicitous Souls.

If Management wants me to **FEAR** them, they'd better get used to being denied with every breath; if I **won't** fear God... what hope does someone in a Suit have? If Fear equals Respect, then I **don't** Respect them. And just as I Papa said would happen: they did *everything* to shake Fear into me.

And the **FEMALES...**; there was **one** who tried to reach the Man struggling beneath mental/emotional trauma. The **rest** were looking for Local Standard: Swinging Dick with a smile and cash; not **one** from that lot made the effort to get to know Who or What I was. So when I shut several down **ruthlessly...**

What's wrong with him? The Answer:

I'm used to different Social Rules... **like don't run your fuckin' mouth about everyone and**

everything, putting your Biz and shit about people you don't even KNOW out for Public Consumption!!!! I'm **really** surprised there aren't **more** shootings over Wandering Dick or Cheating Cunts... not to mention niggas blastin' snitches; there are people **WALKING AND *TALKING LOUDLY*** about how they'll tell ***everything!!!*** None of that shit flies back home in the Big Easy; snitches get Dealt With quick-fast. In Southern Virginia **one** person gets shot and the entire county quakes in naked **TERROR** and starts bitchin' about safety.

But there's a catch: if there is a **known reason/excuse** behind the shooting then ***not one SOUL*** will give two shits. Random Chaos terrifies the Locals; living in some of America's largest, most violent Mega-Cities probably dulled this tendency within me. Then again, I never wasted my time keeping tabs on someone else's life; I was busy trying to figure out why I was the way I was and **improve** myself!!! Born in the Projects, I learned to keep my eyes open and my mouth ***shut***; this was the best way to survive. It also allowed those with sharp, intelligent minds many opportunities to study Human Interaction and Social Rules.

Then there is the Corporation running the Restaurant. I understand the Corp Mindset: *backstab GOD for a better pay grade and Benefits*; in Southern Virginia it mutates into the Personal Fiefdom: secure your Place at **all costs!!!** Not sure about how they train their Managers but the first thing the **General Manager** did was set it up so that the company got a Tax Break from hiring a Hurricane Katrina Victim. I'm not sure about the specifics, but one thing I am sure of: the Corp paid **no taxes** on me by stating on my *OFFICIAL* TAX PAPERS THAT I WAS *married with five kids!!!!!* I'm **still** fighting to recover from the shit they did to my Taxpayer Status *for two years!!!* Worse, this Mentality is **firmly** rooted in more than one managerial employee... *and it gets taught to Newbies!!!*

Got fired from that place; the Manager with the *ain't Redneck Enough* bullshit wouldn't stop with the subtle pokes. I blew up and got fired, but I didn't mind: an Executive Chef I worked for in New Orleans said I would probably get the axe because of some of my Ways. Honest Black Man lookin' to **KEEP** clear of Fed Charges: **God won't *ALLOW*** *such a thing in the South!!!* Black Man more interested in gaining Friends than pussy: *IMPOSSIBLE!!!!* Know my rights and have ZERO problems fighting for them: PROBLEM MAKER!!! Chef warned me about what he called Militant Black Man and it is appropriate his presence makes itself known at this junction.

He has a daughter: beautiful Young Lady *Named AMY...*

I met the Woman who would damn near destroy what little Soul I had left in that particular Corp Kitchen; she followed me to a Proper Kitchen, where our Friendship became something that pushed me to a Place I'd grown tired of visiting: **The Brink of Suicide.**

Yet... there is one good thing about my stint in Corp-Hell: Angels on Earth; I run across them constantly, so encountering **two** in that place was interesting. Especially Sasha; she stood by me during the **entire** shit storm Amy put me through... that I put **myself** through trying to recover from making a mistake I **knew** was one Good Fuck away.

She helped keep me straight; Sasha reminded me about the skills honed in **Fine Dining,** the Skillz learned from Surviving a *serious* Big City Sprawl, and **NEVER** let me forget the Code I still follow.

* * * *

* * * *

The Writer's Soul

I write; during my tenure in the Big Easy it helped relieve Work Stress. Before each shift I'd write, forcing myself to create a small scene before heading into the Kitchen; after each shift I'd do the same. This doesn't mean I didn't experience the Night Life; I simply didn't let my excursion into those shadows dominate or define me any longer than absolutely necessary. I posted most of my stories in my online journal or on a site dedicated to mostly erotic stories; the journal site crashed not long after Hurricane Katrina's devastation, meaning the bulk of my earlier stories are utterly lost.

Upon landing in Southern Virginia I quickly returned to writing; my Thoughts, scattered and bruised by my ordeal, churned within my mind. As I tried coping via writing I watched as my *style* shifted. Where once my stories were Science Fiction and Erotica, the stories became more... **me.** I found another journal site and began posting, though the differences were shockingly obvious; there were few Action-Adventure elements. Indeed, they tended to mirror my emotional instability and deeply introspective side. Even my forays into Sci-Fi held this distinction, culminating in an entire Universe: an on-going series of long and short snippets bathed in odd sexuality/sensuality and Mind-Fucks.

The only constant: I ***never*** shared my writings with those I worked with; within the Kitchen, no Social Activity holds more unnerving power than Writing. Writing required **THOUGHT and *Intelligence***; I made things worse because I'm African American. The stereotype of a Black Author: buzzwords such as *empowerment* and *upliftment*; I classify my stories as **Urban Gothic**. Few understand what this means, though **many** African Americans KNOW the subject all too well: *they're **LIVING** IT*; they reflect what I see happening in The Streets and Da Hood, terminology only glimpsed via Hollywood glamour and Rap Music's darker, emotional lyricists.

I expected rejection from my co-workers, so I never shared my stories; this held true even after

Hurricane Katrina... for a while. The horrors viewed during my three day stay in the Superdome began eroding my Soul, infesting my daily life; from there my stories became rife with twisted emotions and sullen thoughts. Eventually I came to the conclusion that I **had** to share my stories... part of my Existence... with someone; here I ran smack into three decades of paranoia-for-hydraulics powered gates. Only those I trust with my life are allowed so close to me, and those are few and far between. So... find someone. Here... in a place where I was *sure* no such Soul existed.

That's when I encountered Amy. She ran Expo; I'd just worked my way up to being the primary Grill Cook. We became friends slowly, mainly because I refused to trust anyone blindly; she proved to be excellent at her Job, and her Mind wasn't mired in the local quagmire. As I bungled through one maybe-relationship after the next our friendship solidified; hindsight grants me clear vision of this Warning Sign, yet during my tribulations all I knew was this: I'm trying something new and failing miserably.

Then came something which, according to Street Lore, is a Death Knell: she opened up about **her** life. I listened; that is my Nature. I cared; again... that is my Nature: I care for those I call Friend. Yet as we grew closer, old Street Wisdom kept ringing in my ears: *shorty say the nigga dat she wi' ain't shit!!!* I walked a dangerous line, opting to offer an ear as well as compassion; I even believed that my exodus from our mutual Kitchen would be beneficial. I did not expect her to follow me, though when she did... I made a deadly mistake; Good Friends make horrible Lovers.

* * * *

I am a damaged, broken thing; I accept this as Fact because to do otherwise is to lie to myself, and that I cannot do... ever. Working six years in Kitchens where everything I loathe about my chosen profession is neatly bundled beneath Corporate profit mongering nearly crushed my spirit; dealing with fake smiles and smooth backstabbing pats on the back only fueled the crippling paranoia I've lived with my entire life. And then... there's Amy.

I find myself thinking on her from time to time, and I ask myself, "Do you still Love her?" Yes or No would be much easier if Hate filled the void left by her passage; it does not... because I've spent countless hours battling its rotten Essence, forcing myself to see where I screwed up. Facing Inner Demons is never easy and I do it constantly; it doesn't matter that I no longer see her or communicate with her, this Demon will rear its hideous face every time I see some beautiful Woman and feel the aches and debilitating suffering my decades of Solitude leave upon my deflated, crumbled Soul. I crave the warmth Love offers, yet cannot shake the eternal cold I know lies deep within these ancient bones: I will never Know Love... at least as others define it.

I cannot say I love her; I cannot say I despise her very existence. I learned much from this mistake, and **re-learned** some valuable Street Lessons. **NEVER** love with all you have; it leaves nothing left *when* you loose it. I learned that I am truly evil, for when Nothing sparked into being within my frame it was because Nothing is all I will ever be; I am Nothing, and that is beyond any evil imaginable. There is no cold spite or savage-red anger festering within my body; there is no kindness to my Thoughts... no compassion to warm my heart. Indeed, that vibrant organ does not beat within my chest; there is only Nothing. She should be proud; none before her can lay claim to hindering my progress Forward for such a long time. None before her can puff out their chest and croon, "I have destroyed what little goodness resided within that foul thing *daring* to call itself **Man**."

*And perhaps she should be afraid. I am true to one thing and one thing only; **I Follow a Code.** Yes I am broken. Yes I will remain forever Nothing. I will **not** stay down however; **Always Forward... Always Onward**. Perhaps she should fear the unholy thing rising from the cesspool and detritus of what once was; perhaps she **does** fear the unloving thing dragging along the ground, rising with aching slowness and damnation-empowered determination. Fear me, for I am Nothing. I cannot care. I cannot hate. I cannot love. I Exist. Whatever the Challenge I will face it without Human emotions; I will not care for the innocent lives caught in the battle's raging* *madness. I will not seek victory. I will not care if I survive.*

I know who I can trust, and they are my Strength. Gripped by depression, desperation ground down into savage, primal determination, I chose to believe in what I knew.

* * * *

It had to happen... if I didn't end up eating the business end of a .45 first. Strangely... it happened when I was stone sober.

One day I dragged my ass out of bed after two months packed with nightmares and strange dreams; truth be told I wasn't tired despite the exhaustion gripping my muscles. I was just... **here**; I looked around my room slowly, sniffing the furnace-warmed air. I got up and dressed for another stressful day sitting in front of my monitor; I had ten documents open and each one needed serious work before the stories within their words were satisfactory. I nuked the dregs from last nights coffee, re-up the coffee flow without much fanfare, and scratch out breakfast: blueberry bagel and cream cheese; old coffee inhaled quickly I sauntered into the living room and flipped channels until the fresh coffee smell slapped the last dream remnants from my brain. New mug in one hand... breakfast balanced in the other, I returned to my cave and wolfed down my fare; occasionally I'd flip up one document and dabble-edit, and in one case the dabble sealed the deal nicely, connecting several scenes better than my notes scripted.

"Now for the real shit," I sighed. Spark up the Black & Mild after my third cup of morning and...

I sat in front of my monitor. I did **not** feel darkness; I did not want to swallow and regurgitate depressing Thoughts. I glanced at the small clock on my computer desk, surprised by how *early* it was: 08:03; I **never** get up this early unless I have a shitload of writing to do or a job interview to prep for, so I sat there trying to force the stories. Never a good idea; I kept drifting off, my Thoughts going anywhere and everywhere... except for two places: that vile cesspool filled with Depression... **and Amy**. After downing my coffee I grabbed a lighter and my cigarillo and headed outside; maybe I just needed to clear my head.

Instead... I found myself choking on the crisp near-Winter chill; a patrol car crept by, and I got Stink-Eye from the passenger-side Assassin. The car slowed down for one heartbeat, then sped up; I smirked: they probably checked the address and wanted **zero** to do with me after I'd vehemently defended my Civil Rights the *last* time one of their viral strain decided he needed his Nigga Notch. Aside from that brief reminder of why I desperately **NEEDED** to get the fuck out of this bullshit town, I actually enjoyed the morning!!! I even felt the faint warmth as the sun raced towards its zenith; that hadn't happened for longer than I cared to remember. But the best thing about my outside adventure was the *very* faint moan deep within the void where my Soul once rested whenever I thought about Amy; memories of her are faded, phantasmal maybes, each quickly replaced by the stinging thoughts of former acquaintances, betrayals and other foul memories of my stay here. And with each memory I found myself caring less and less about the people involved; with each memory a cold thing grew warm within me.

Not Anger... not Rage; before Hurricane Katrina kicked me out of my Home I was ready for Tomorrow. Since then my only claim to fame is publishing one book which has only slightly disturbed the populace and brought **very little** financial gain. It **did** leave me with the confidence to keep writing and hone my skills; it gave me something to do when the only thing I wanted was Death's icy clutches strangling Life from my body. That cold thing is Tomorrow and the unknown it wields with savage brutality; I understand **that**, the cruel uncertainty of keeping one step ahead of Death. Here... I sit and wait for the Eternal Foe.

I returned to my room, making sure to lock the front door; inside my bedroom I stared at the screen saver. I hadn't been on Facebook for several weeks and didn't expect anyone to notice; so imagine my surprise when I saw the small plethora of notices and messages. For a moment I smiled; it faded instantly as I recalled **who** had access to my site. I pulled an old-school Kick-Ban-Block on Amy; the only way she had access was through Public Posts (maybe) and the few mutual associates. Even then I expected her intel to be limited to gossip and rumor and complete bullshit conjecture. Sighing heavily I opened the message lists; I wasn't disappointed: not **one** associate or mutual acquaintance spared me even a simply hello.

However... more than one contact from my Big Easy days dropped a line; this included, "Whaddup Nig!!" from one guy named Big Slick. He's a true 504 Thug OG; above him were two others from New Orleans and each message, though short, pulled my smile wider. Then the message bar winked into existence: Sasha.

Sir?

Greetings Little One; how are you?

Fine Sir; how are you?

Not sure...

hugs

She reminds me: not *everything* about this shit hole was negative. She also reminds me of just how twisted I am, and I am thankful for this reminder. I'm not better, just alive-and-kickin'; so long as that's true I can **maybe** cling to that last shred of Hope a few people claim will keep a person safe.

* * * *

* * * *

I met Sasha around the same time Amy and I began our loosely defined Workplace Friendship. Ours was, by Local Standards, a Proper Interracial Friendship; we never met where her friends or family could encounter us. Not that we were hiding anything, and we most certainly were **not** romantically involved; our Friendship began by accident. I overheard her talking about writing poetry and asked if she'd ever been published; I mentioned my writings and Friendship sparked... though she warned me: *I tend to be a bit dark and graphic.* Indeed, our writing styles are **very** similar; she displayed great talent and passion in her works.

Perhaps my recent dark turn helped me notice certain similarities between her poems and short stories and her Reality; they **definitely** sharpened my awareness of things around her. At first she appeared to be soft-spoken, quintessential Good Girl from the South; yet I could not shake Thoughts of Gothic Lady. While uncommon, such a blend is not impossible; there are jokes about Country Music being depressing... similar to the darkened aspects of melodic Goth Music in my opinion. Studying her writings yielded troubles with Scum.

I am a Dom; the Lifestyle, BDSM, is part of my
Life. Sasha is submissive. Yet I avoided twisting our
friendship into something fueled by those black
passions; what I did not expect was our friendship to
find firm Foundation upon another aspect of my
Existence: my adherence to a Code. It is similar to
the Code of the Samurai, yet vastly different in that it,
like me, is forged within the Streets. Sasha found
this fascinating, just as she found it curious that I
loved wolves, a love she carries very close to her
Heart. What does this have to do with the Lifestyle?

She dated a scumball who **dared** use the
Dominant/submissive Relationship to justify how he
treated her. I remember the first time I saw him;
everything about him screamed scumbag. He
lounged near the bar area, his posture at odds with
the Dominant air he gave off by running his mouth.
At first I didn't know he **was** her boyfriend; another
server let that slip. I never let on that I knew **why** she
found him enticing; I've known more than one
submissive Female attracted to cowards cloaked in
false Dominant mannerisms. Eventually she brought
up their relationship, doing so in a manner I thought
odd at the time: she asked for Solace.

What happens or is Spoken here, **STAYS
HERE**; this is my Way, offered **only** to someone I
trust. We spoke at length about the Lifestyle, and I
was struck by how easily she accepted the fact that
I'm a Dom; when I asked her about that, Sasha
smiled softly. I will always remember that Smile; it

came from her Soul, bathing already beautiful features in gentle blue-white warmth. Sasha never asked for anything, not even advice; she talked, something her boyfriend **never** allowed; and I listened as her Thoughts and Emotions rushed from her lips. I did not judge her actions; I never offered a Comment unless she asked for it. Even then, she only asked, "What do you think?" I always spoke honestly, something she apparently never got from his sorry ass. It was during her first visit that she asked about Amy.

"Are you seeing her?"

"No," I sighed.

"Oh... sorry..."

"No, Sasha; I know she's got an Ol' Man. I'm just... concerned about what I See before me." She remained silent; I emptied my small glass spoon and packed another bowl. As I took a hit she spoke, her voice soft yet firm:

"Has your Gift ever been wrong?"

"Unfortunately: never; **this** is why I am worried. Part of me *wants* to be wrong, hun; but I've learned the hard way: dismissing its Wisdom will not end favorably." I snort a chuckle, my gaze lingering on the dying ember surrounded by blackened resin. "When it comes to Matters of the Heart, I am a poor Judge."

"Remember what you told me? *If you are too close, Step Back.*"

"There's a flaw in that. Judging ones own actions may have some Wisdom, but is seldom accurate. It helps to have someone you Trust... someone capable of keeping **their** Heart out of the equation; finding such a Soul is often difficult."

"May I offer my eyes?" Her next words held my attention because of their soothing honesty: "You've given freely to me: your time... patience... an ear..."

I place the glass spoon on my computer desk, turned to face the stunningly beautiful, quiet Woman seated on my bed, and broke a Personal Rule: *never* talk about one Female to **another** Female, especially when they work together or are otherwise in direct contact. I cannot blame anything I'd experienced, not even Hurricane Katrina, for my actions; I knew I trusted Sasha.

* * * *

Amy won't speak to me unless I speak first, though she calls me Friend; can't hang out with her unless it's done secretly, far away from anyone who knows her or her Significant Other. I am now her Dirty Little Secret... and the Dick in the Glass Case; her Ol' Man. starts fucking up and I **used** to hear every sordid detail; but the moment I showed genuine concern for her Feelings I became the Dick in the Glass Case, the shoulder to cry on while she stroked my crotch.

When things began improving in her relationship I found myself completely cut off; if I don't speak to her during the course of Work I don't hear a damned thing except grinding silence. This tainted everything; even insignificant bullshit became the fucking Himalayan Mountains. During this time I spent many hours talking to Sasha, though I noticed *she* confined our talks to online chats... except for once; I remember opening the door, pleased for the company.

Then I saw the tears. I remember asking her if something was wrong with her grandmother (suffering from cancer); I also remember the expression on her face: *I wish...* She unzipped her pink hoodie, wincing as she tried to pull it off. In that instant Amy ceased to be anything; less than a heartbeat later I saw the bruises on her arm. All I remember after that: white-hot Rage.

"Please... don't..." Sasha stared at me; I burned my gaze through her tears.

"Stay inside and lock the door." She didn't try to stop me.

She never asked why her boyfriend dumped her on the phone about two hours later; the strained terror in his voice... the choking gasps... offered all answers. I looked rather distressed *physically*; my face betrayed the Truth of my Soul: Cold... devoid of compassion - the Face of the **Demon**. I set about washing my clothes, which is how I heard the outside water running. I'd left my shoes on the concrete walkway; I looked outside and saw Sasha carefully washing my shoes. "They'll need to be replaced," she spoke evenly.

"Eventually," I replied. I studied her closely; her body held a quiet calm in its crouched posture.

"I'm being foolish if I give him another chance."

"It could prove fatal." Though my words held Wisdom's Tone, there was nothing Human within them.

"I understand," she sighed after a *long*, thoughtful pause. Then: "May I stay here tonight? I feel safe here."

"You will always be Safe here, Little One." I returned to the washroom. Something had... **evolved** between Sasha and I; it occupied my Thoughts as I went about my task. It felt different than the chaotic mess that was Amy, and there was also the very ominous Sense of *something is missing*. It would take months before I understood: the Demon was replaced by The Master, my Dominant persona... and a part of me long dormant.

BLOW THE END

"Yo D, you ridin' wit tonight?"

"Who Drivin'."

"Mike 'n me; got some kill and a blunt."

"Do dat; lemme Close this bitch down proper."

* * * *

Recession; good if you car pool to and from work; here... it's one way for Cooks to unwind: Ridin'... Cruisin' to Old Folks. Mike ain't drinkin tonight; can't quite fight the heartburn; good thing: One-Times are out in force. Of course, I knew that from the gunplay that popped off at the ass-end of the night; too much stupidity out-and-about; this will be about a half-blunt Roll.

Once we were away from the Kitchen and inside People Land (aka: **Normalcy**), the bass thumped just loud enough to let the Hoods recognize; we dipped to a few Spots to check out this and that, swapping music and life info and raucous bullshit for a few as we quietly puffed on the one blunt. We maintained Cypher, passing the blunt to the left until every head was truly High and all felt good; however we never talked about work, including the servers.

But music? We Listened, finding the grooves easily; occasionally we'd spit along with the Lyrics and comment on styles and which Rapper/MC we thought was the best; there was no Ad-lib: that is strictly to remove Workplace Stress while on the Line. My place was first on the return loop, and I was glad for the swift-yet-pleasant Session. It helps solidify the Bond between the Cooks participating, but after the Bond is strengthened I prefer quiet time... alone or with my Ol' Lady. I don't roll with the dish crew mainly because they will eventually get into some *real* Dirt after a shift; my Nights in **that** Game are over... and I prefer Doin' Dirt in the Big Easy. There are fewer loose lips eager to blab there.

* * * *

* * * *

"We good?"

"Yeah... just tell the Servers to hurry up!!"

"Done. **LET'S ROLL!!**" Kilo and I don't bother looking at each other; we can already taste the alcohol and blunt-smoke, Ghostly over the other Kitchen flavors dangling over our tongues.

And I'm Still Hungry; there is much Prey here... **WILLING** *Prey.*

Damn good thing I'm sober and closing this puppy down for the night; gonna work on organizing a Book, my first, and while I really *could* use a quickie, they have a bad habit of following a nigga Home and Talkin' Stupid: *cuddling and Pillow Tale are for my Ol' Lady,* **NOT** *the Bitch I just dropped a load in/on!!!*

"Babygirl... it was *just* good, kinky Sex; keep it there and we'll be fine. Fuck with my Money by bringin' that shit into the Workplace and I'll Disavow everything, ya 'eard me?" Doesn't matter how many times they hear this... doesn't matter if God-Almighty were to say it: *they won't buy it!!!* If you take time during sex, it automatically means Emotional Attachment; it doesn't even matter if you're like me: pushin' forty and nowhere **near** over-eager Youngster *slangin' Big Dick all-Night Long.* You risk Emotional Attachment even if you just feel like taking your time and **ENJOYING** THE SEX!!! Personally, I ain't got time to entertain your Goo-Goo Eyes and **won't** whisper those Pretty Lies and Promises those young cats *abuse* in the Game; when I start talking like that: Bankable... better than Bible, hun. Yes I am a Freak; I am also much more: **ARE YOU?**

And while I'm on this whole O.G. Pimplicious-meets-Hood Gothic Mentality... there are three lesbian servers I'd like to discus. One is on her way out: pissed on too many people I guess; the other two are familiar **if** I got by my past experiences. Joy (white) is, in my experience, Trouble Waiting; Rain (black) is Bisexual with Heavy Lesbian Tendencies. This is as far as my Knowledge goes because of the Panty Rule: ***Any Male Speaking to a Female is***

gunnin' for the Pussy. Can't just *wanna hang and blow two* with them because they have good taste in music, we share similar Movie interests... and they can't ask about my stories. Why? **Panty Rule for Lesbians:** ***if you're talking to anything with a Penis, you're looking to try the Other Side.*** Friendship with the Opposite Sex is out-of-the-Question, and this is killing my Social Circle. And I can't blame the Local Mentality on this bullshit; every Kitchen I've been in has it to some degree.

Although... maybe it's better to say that Society in general has the Panty Rule; that makes more sense, and ain't the least bit comforting: Stupidity Knows No Boundaries/Limitations. Scary Thought; I take another puff from the blunt and Shoot Shit with Kilo as we cruise the back streets, tunes bumpin' and brains oozing as we try to forget the crap we call Work.

"Ay yo... Rocco says you got all dem readin' yo shit, D."

"Really?"

"Yep; caught a few of 'em... *stuck* to their phones, Cuz!!" I laugh, filing away the information as my High rolls quietly behind eyes constantly scanning for Assassins.

"How many new hostesses we got anyhow?!?! Had some new chic **challenge** a nigga when I bounced in today..."

"WHAA...?"

With the local High School in session we get more than a few Sixteen-Year-Old Hot Bodies (hey... blame management for the selection!!) working the front door. Each one comes in and looks around, eye bright with mischief; you can blame Hollywood for painting Cook in certain lights, but I see something else: a shitload of young Females with **way** too much Street Savvy for their outward appearance looking for a walk on the Wild Side... where *all* Cooks are said to linger. Toss in the tatted-up ones with *serious* Hardness in their eyes and stance and it makes a nigga wonder what White Middle-Class America is bringing up in Bible-fed Country Livin'/Country Music Lovin' America: **most of these Looks belong on Hood Rats, seasoned Gold Diggers and HOES!!!** And when a few of their non-white peers give 'em scowls of Street Respect/Female Playa Hatin'-followed-by-Fake-Ass-Smile/Polite: **Game Recognizes Game** and I'm forced to look beyond the overly Doll-Cute face and any Posture quirks.

I'm looking for Street Mentality: Dark and Twisted, yet flavored by Upbringing: Your Hood... My Hood; in some hoods, Country Music instead of curse word bloated, bass heavy Rap is the Sound. And I'm finding myself less and less surprised to see/know/hear of the same cute, innocent face Doin' Dirt; *she doesn't smoke, she's a Supa-Chief... she's a lush and'll drink ya under ANY table...*; you spew the Gossip and I've come across a racially diverse version of the Good Girl/Guy, and more often than not there are more Shadows and skeletons than any graveyard anywhere.

"And what about 'Chelle and dat **azz!!!**"

"Don't remind me," I laugh. She's Barely Legal: eighteen; she *looks* fifteen and has a high-pitched voice to match. Listen to the words and her tone, however, and I'd place her as just another wannabe Skripper-Ho wandering the French Quarter. What's worse is that Kilo is absolutely right; her ass **SCREAMS**: Bite Me... Suckle upon these wondrous globes of flesh.

She teases, and that's a plus; she Works her body as a Dancer would, and the other servers are silently jealous, forcing Kilo, myself and the other cooks to lavish *extra* attention to **avert** Target Fixation... and in the Process, we select our Stables. All Cooks have Stables of servers; they work *very* well with them and are often seen joking with them if Out-and-About. This is true for every Kitchen... but there's a Problem: FREAKS.

Hang with Freaks in *any* Bible-Belt Town and you *ADD* to your **FAMILY'S** Rep. Gossip moves faster than light.

* * * *

* * * *

Back in my flop I set myself up to put the finishing touches on another Story. I check Facebook... and smile oddly at one particular Female on my Friends List; she's African American, a **proud** Black Woman, one of the *precious FEW* near my age. I knew her from Back-in-the-Day. Wouldn't approach her then and won't now; I can blame the marijuana I smoke, since that **is** why Humans have Crutches. But the Truth is, I just ain't Worthy; call it Upbringing or Tradition, I will never have what it takes to 'get' someone like that. Never mind this oddity: *I can See her Making Love... but **FUCKIN'? NOPE!!!*** It may sound odd, but Passion is **confined** to Love Making with her and similar Black Females.

I rather like **LEAVING** things right there; I don't like thinking she's seen enough Darkness and Pain to be Beneath My Hand or any other Dom. She doesn't have *submissive* anywhere in her gaze or stance. Tenderness is a Given: *she's Female!!!* But I cannot picture her yielding enough Control to enjoy raw, dangerous Passion... and **that** is what I require. So I'll ponder why she reads my stories, not completely comfortable with simple intellectual interest and unsatisfied with *she's curiously fascinated.* She **IS** a Woman, ethnicity be shit on by a flock of geese, so I leave my guesses floating; I blaze until they evaporate, replaced by proper chaos and chemical happiness.

From Human cometh Foundation, and every Human *alive* has felt Arousal; what they've done to

Deal with it is Personal. This offends the current *I-Must-know-EVERYTHING-you- do/think* Mentality. So... if you **must** know everything: **SHE GETS HORNY TOO!!!** How she Deals with it: ***PERSONAL!!!***

It is up to me to get over feeling like a Dirty Little Secret and just accept her and those like her; be a shitload easier if I were published **and** Famous: **then** she'd look ***SMART*** and ahead-of-her-Times (like she *should, by Upper-Crust Bougie African American Standards*). And no matter how rich either of us gets: I write Erotica; by Local Standards, you **must** keep such things tucked *far* within the darkest corner of your Closet. Problem: I **will** be beyond Famous; hard to keep even feigned interest in such Things/Ideas quiescent/concealed once the ever-present Public Eye-Camera focuses on you..

* * * *

* * * *

As far as Endings go, this was straight forward; then I checked my messages on Facebook... and things went a bit... well...

Yasmine is a Strong Black Female; I'd call her Woman, but according to **my** Definition, that means she's a Freak when the Doors and Blinds close. She asked me to attend a function going down in town; I agreed, *warning* her that I wasn't a good dancer; this is Big Easy Speak for **Ain't My Style.**

Which isn't a complete lie; I enjoy dancing, but there's something about putting too many Black Folk together. Black Folk become **Niggas** with too much alcohol and too many Egos; toss in tits shaking and butts bouncin' for a highly volatile concoction within a confined space. Add tempers for combustion source and...: **NIGGAS!!!!** With Yasmine as my apparent Date, heads were guaranteed to turn; New Orleans was Out and About, and that's the polite Name for me. Still, I do enjoy getting Fresh-and-Clean for a Night Out with a very attractive Woman.

Yeah... Woman; and *technically* this is a Date. That means I blaze myself senseless before a hot bath, while drying off and selecting my Gear for the evening. **THAT** part of me is working overtime: Street Warrior; I can't outshine Yasmine, but I can't be so dull as to **not** attract some other bit of fluff lookin' to vulture a penis for the evening. Also, I can't look like a complete bum or appear to have zero Fashion Sense; that means pretending that I give a shit about what someone else thinks about my appearance.

And in the end, the only thing that happens worthy of Note and Notice?

Most of the other African American Females tended to ignore me; I didn't Look and Smell like Money (Legit or *otherwise...*), so they watched Yasmine to see how she acted around me. When that didn't give them a clear indication of Who I Was to her: watch and whisper. This is **not** the place for any naturally paranoid Soul, much less one raised with Street Warrior instincts and mentality. It wasn't long before all I wanted was to step outside, find the darkest corner drenched in the deepest shadow, spark-up and drift away; why? **I'd come to Da Club Naked:** *unarmed for those who don't know Street Law.*

The next week **ends** the same, right down to the Facebook Message source; *content* changed, and that altered the rest of the Story... ***drastically.***

She showed up with a six-pack of hard cider, looking about as Street Casual as her wardrobe would allow; that meant there wasn't excess gold dripping from fingers, hanging around her neck and/or dangling from her ears, just simple gold hoop earrings and a favorite ring sparkling on one finger. Her hair was stylish, and *definitely* held distinct Street Edge: Sex Hair - if it got fucked up during sex she wasn't out any money. She wasn't expecting Sex despite the matching outfit, the Hair and bling-free body accessories; she expected *something*, but like many others in her place, she had no idea **WHAT** to expect, other than seeing me buzzed.

And in that, she expected me to be silly or glued to a video game; when I turned out to be a Good Host (as defined by those within her Circle and Local Standards), she flat out asked me about the marijuana. From that moment on, she isn't Local Female: she's just another Woman who doesn't understand the guy standing/sitting before them... not at all. I wasn't Thug-on-the-Prowl-fo'-Pussy; I *definitely* wasn't Stoner too blitzed to hold a logical, intelligent, coherent conversation. She even remarked that she'd never seen me **SMILE** as much; she betrayed her Thoughts as she stared at me: I was... odd.

Just... odd.

So I smile Honestly and talk to her; when she leaves, I notice that it takes her the distance to her car and several quiet moments before the Local Mask is back in place and she reaches for her Smart Phone. She glances up at me, a movement she can't know I see given the dark shadows concealing my features, not to mention I'm turned to head back inside; still... it reminds me of someone peeking over a veil, a playful smile dancing behind her eyes before Strong Black Woman who would **never** be seen with Street Scum like me is back in place.

I'd laugh... if it was funny or unexpected.

* * * *

* * * *

Of the Females I've encountered here, only Sasha and Amy never gave me Shit about Smoking Bud; Black Females tend to come in two distinct Flavors: Old School and New Jack.

Old School Black Females *always* turn their noses up the instant they catch a whiff of marijuana;

New Jacks won't bat an eye. **They'll assume you know the Rules:** *Social Marijuana Use!!*

1)   Ask before you Spark up in their presence; unless you're at Da Club or House Party hosted by someone else.

2)   Ask before you Blaze inside their vehicle; if they are Passenger in your Ride, ask pardon before you spark.

3)   *Leave no Evidence!!!*

Follow those Rules of Social Graces and you Mark yourself **Respectful Pothead**; believe it or not, this is actually a crucial Step towards being Thought of as *MAN* within New Jack's Mind.

* * * *

* * * *

Shitty Nights *will* happen. Back home I'd bounce around the French Quarter until my Mood improved, **even when I lived alone**; there's no need to bring home ten tons of negative attitude. I've had my share and will continue to have them if I continue my Career.

One Shitty Night happened when a Female Manager asked if I had some paperwork for her. I didn't, and there's a damned good Reason for my actions: the Restaurant wanted me to sign a paper giving Management the **RIGHT** to poke their fuckin' noses into my Facebook site *for the purposes of seeing if I'd posted any Company Recipes... **OR ANYTHING PERTAINING TO THAT PLACE!!!*** Fuck that shit; most of my stories centered around a **Professional Cook!!!** I know enough about people in this town to understand just how shit **WILL** get blown out of proportion, not to mention knowing *which* assumptions will be made and **WHO** will make them; I have a saying that covers this: ***Don't stick ya Dick into a Meat Grinder; the end result is guaranteed to HURT and leave a bloody fuckin' mess.*** So I told her **before this incident**: not gonna sign something that effectively means giving up my First Amendment Rights.

She asked for the paperwork when the **only** thing in my head was Kitchen; I'd left the paper at home, and I'd been rearranging my room. So... **stop** thinking about Work and *remember* where I'd last seen that one slip of paper **in a PILE of papers**; apparently taking time to recall a damned thing upset her... **and she decides to snap her fingers in front of my face!!!!**

Within the Lifestyle this is a Sign of Ownership. My eyes darted towards the stupid cunt and I felt my body tense; to this day I say God Almighty stayed my hand. Otherwise her newborn child would be motherless; I had every intention of choking her out, bashing her head against the concrete wall until I could open her skull like a cracked egg. **NOT** the attitude *anyone* should possess, especially working the Line on a busy Friday Night; I jerked another Manager into the office, let them know **just how on edge and dangerous** I was because of that ho's arrogant gesture. I'm a Dom; Knowing ones Place is vital. I **work** for the company; *NO ONE OWNS ME AND ANYONE WHO MAKES THE ATTEMPT TO DO SO THROWS THEIR LIFE AWAY!!!!!!*

Did she apologize? She's still breathing, so the answer is No; I tend to take Lord Vader's view on How to Accept Apologies: *when you're dead at my feet; not before!!*

Worst part of this: every other Female within my eyesight has to deal with me when I can't Think of them as anything other than Two-Tits-and-a-Twat; that's as close as I can get to Thinking of them as Human. I make it through my shift... somehow; as soon as I'm outside and off the clock I fire up the partial Black & Mild I'd tucked in my backpack.

"Sir?" I turn around slowly; naked Rage tightens my shoulders.

"If you'll wait ten minutes I'll give you a ride, Sir."

I accept with a curt nod... **because Sasha's posture is *perfectly* submissive!!!**

* * * *

Never fuck with a Nigga's Money, **especially** come time for his first Paid Vacation *ever!!!* I'd filled out the necessary paperwork; I double-checked to make **sure** I'd timed things right: **NO Money!!!!**

Most will say calm, level-headed Methods work best with Corporate Types; they're probably right in the end... but this wasn't the first time they'd fucked up my paycheck. In fact, it seemed to be a common *theme* for no less than five months: **someone** didn't get paid on time or got shorted. I'd had enough; I blew through the empty dining area hell-bent on leaving with one of two things: m'Money or someone's Life. Hadn't felt like that since I left those Big Easy Nights chasing some ho, and it wasn't a side of me Amy had the pleasure of witnessing before.

Part of her recoiled in utter horror; some dark corner got aroused (I recognized her faint smile). Then a female Manager with big tits and her standard loose-fitting cleavage-showing blouse tried Tit-Bounce-and-Smile: guaranteed to soothe the Savage Beast... right? Swap Swinging Dick for Savage Beast and her technique works; heartless Hood-raised Nigga lookin' for his Money, only to discover a pair of TITS bouncing in his face and plump, recently moistened lips smiling at him and *NO* Dead Presidents?

"WHERE M'MONEY!!!!"

Yes I got paid; I also got stink-eye from Amy... and a text: *Go home and get high.* First pseudo-conversation from her in just under three months;

the **only** Reason I didn't open my mouth: **I had m'Money in my Hand.**

* * * *

* * * *

Amy likes drinking; she's no lush however. Drinking is her Vice of Choice; I prefer Tokin' Up. Sasha's Vice: Cooking; all Vice stems from Stress and how Humans cope.

Amy reminded me of someone from the Big Easy; both Females wondered why I *never* went out in public unless I was buzzed. Amy didn't stick around long enough to understand: my answer isn't bullshit - I have an ***extremely*** low acceptance for Stupid. For example: the so-called Parents pushing a child in a stroller **DOWN BOURBON STREET AT NIGHT!!!!! *ON A WEEKEND PACKED WITH DRUNKEN COLLEGE KIDS, TOURISTS AND LOCALS RUNNIN' HUSTLES?!?!?!?*** What in the name of all that's Holy were they thinking? Turns out **Normal** People are *allowed* Moments of Insanity like that; even now I do not understand. Wearing a Polo shirt and khakis, clad in a stylish dress or skirt or slacks... wearing a fashionable blouse with perfectly chosen accessories: these convey upon one the Power to simply ignore Common Sense and Human Decency. Utter nonsense, but... **those with Money make the Rules**; they are also the *only* ones allowed to break said rules with impunity. To me:

Stupidity; Amy never understood my way of thinking.

Sasha understood; so did my companion back Home in New Orleans. Normal People, when viewing something stupid, laugh and shrug it off; if I'm supposed to do this, **I need to be High.** It offsets my sober tendency towards savage, ruthless cruelty when faced with overwhelming stupidity. Sober I'd scowl and sneer, and it would not take long before I opened my mouth and said something guaranteed to piss someone off; High I could smile through things. Even better, it took most of the sting from my razor sharp tongue and the words it formed; that blissed-out Stoner Smile is as close as I come to putting on that plastic Mask called Politeness or *keeping a Civil Tongue*.

THE DEMON'S FINAL BREATH

This is where I'm *supposed* to state some grand epiphany; this is where Closure happens. I have Issues with this concept; I don't believe things really **end**. They simply move on without your immediate influence.

* * * *

Amy said something like this: *I tend to destroy the men in my life.* I remember smiling as I burned her words into Permanent Memory; I also remember my reply: *I tend to find a way through walls and into the Soul.* It was the most honest words Amy and I ever spoke to each other. I don't know if I left a mark on her Soul, but I am all too certain her words were accurate.

I never shed a single tear when we parted ways; instead I sat and shook, Anger boiling into seething Rage and self-loathing bubbling from depths I though were long filled and forgotten. Depression eventually calmed the tumultuous substance, chilling my Soul beyond sub-zero; suicidal thoughts returned, eager to send my Soul screaming straight into Satan's waiting talons. When I do come across Moments of Happiness they are always the same: I'm walkin' through Da Hood with a hoodie and my eyes flipping over potential hiding spots where some fool might lay in wait for another victim.

I can't shake Who and What I Am, and I **am** a Street Samurai. I cannot deny Honor; it kept me alive during Nights back home... long, cold Nights where I *BEGGED* God to end my life. I went sober for six months, hoping **that** would be a start... but start *what* is the question. It didn't help; Depression quickly claimed the void Delta-9 left and it won't let go. So I sat in my flop and stared at Death, demanding it do its Duty and end my pathetic Life; along with writing, I cooked, piddling around with recipes I'd learned or researched online.

That's when I first felt alive: I had eight inches of steel in my hands; even though it wasn't in a Professional Kitchen I felt something thud/thump inside my chest... precisely where my Heart once beat. It's also when I realized Amy was wrong; she didn't destroy me *completely*, though **OTHERS** did their damned level best to finish what she...; I want to say *started*, but she didn't start the erosion I now see and cannot stop. That started the day I set foot back in Southern Virginia. On the day I felt I had no choice but to abandoned my Home and Love: The Kitchen, I began rotting away inside; it doesn't matter that I had no House to return to, I'd left **MY HOME** behind. **THAT** is the root cause of every foul Thought eating what passes for my Soul; the rest is little more than excess rainfall on already water-bloated soil. That includes Amy: one more Storm to weather.

If I keep living I'll eventually run across Death; begging won't get Death's attention any faster, and I still believe in something greater. I have no **CLUE** what that something is, but that's OK. I'll suffer from Depression until I draw my last breath; I can deal with that. It's just another gust of hurricane force winds on my chest; occasionally I'll be blown off my feet and dragged along the cement and asphalt. I'll get scuffed up and scarred, but the winds won't always blow; so long as I'm breathing I'll fight to get to my feet. If this sounds like shiny motivation then so be it; I happen to know the truth. I'll get up because I'm a stubborn bastard... and that wind is just gathering another breath.

* * * *

Another day; I roll my shoulders, groaning softly as Age-sore muscles grudgingly accept Morning awareness and energy. Numbers flip across my Mind's Eye and I quickly reach for the small alarm clock, silencing it before the shrill digital screech awakens that foul, ever-Angry inner demon. I zombie-stumble into the kitchen and prep the inexpensive coffee maker, raising one eyebrow slightly when my brain recognizes the blissful scent from a freshly opened bag of dark roast; *twelve minutes* echoes in my Thoughts, so I trudge into the bathroom to relieve myself. It doesn't take twelve minutes, but I do my best Thinking in the head; I check today's schedule, running the times over and over as I inspect the tub haphazardly. Business concluded I wash my hands, dry them thoroughly, and return to my bedroom; I don't sit down in front of my computer as I clear the screen saver and select Morning Music. I ponder checking my email, the news and other online dalliances until my brain registers the scent of fresh coffee. I move into the kitchen, still slightly hunched over from my hesitation; I don't straighten up until my midnight black coffee mug is filled with steaming black gold.

That first sip; I hiss/yowl like a dragon yawning. Even though I'm squinting things suddenly snap into bright, clear focus. I stop in front of my bedroom door and take two deep gulps; Mental Gears grind and whir as caffeine makes its way through brain cells. I take a seat before my computer monitor, place my mug within easy reach and take several moments to simply enjoy the sensation as my Thoughts slough off sluggishness. Once they reach Normal drudgery I know it's time, and I reach for the small glass spoon resting on top of Blunt Station Zero; I take one long, slow, *deep* pull and hold the smoke until **all** of my muscles get their Delta-9 morning quota. After a small coughing fit I reach for the partial cigarillo sitting in the glass ash tray; I change hands when my Brain screams for more caffeine. I return the cigarillo to its place as I sit back and sip on the rapidly cooling coffee. My gaze lingers on the small glass bowl and its powerful contents; I haven't been Thrice-Baked for nearly five months, and I'd forgotten just how much I enjoy being Baked Silly.

After several minutes I fire up the cigarillo and dive into the electronic ether; email comes first, and there are no real surprises there: advertisements and special offers only. Nothing from Friends or Family: the norm for over a year now; Facebook is similarly depressing, and I quickly leave the social networking site in favor of seriously depressing News. It isn't long before I've killed the cigarillo; I light its replacement and have two drags before closing my browser. Smoke hovers in front of my eyes as I reach for my mug, quaffing the lukewarm dregs without fanfare; I glower into the empty mug before returning to the kitchen for a re-up, the new cigarillo dangling between my frowning lips. I nuke the new cup more to add *time* to the coffee's heat; Winter's chill eats through the comfortable warmth within the place all too easily. I jack the thermostat up, swinging my ears towards the nearest vent as the furnace roars softly. The cigarillo is dead by now; I drop the pinky finger thumbnail-sized ash into the living room trashcan before returning to my bedroom. I spark up the cigarillo and take two pulls before placing it in the ashtray's rest; I yawn, the need for another hit from my bowl gnawing at my neck. Instead of blazing up I flop down in my executive's chair, drink coffee and listen to music until the tips of my ears warm up. Time for a bath.

* * * *

I dry off rapidly, ending the entire process in my bedroom; while removing the wax from my ears I nuke my coffee, listening to the furnace breathe. Before the timer dings I retrieve my mug; it burns my hands... and I enjoy the sensation as Pain flows through neurons. My smile doesn't fade when I set the hot ceramic on the countertop; I hold it in place and search for the Thirst for Life within my Thoughts. It isn't there; my smile jerks into The Joker's cruel grin just long enough to remind me of the Days and Nights when I used to give a shit about *something*.

Back in the Day, this is when I'd sigh heavily and mutter, "I need a hit." There's more than enough Kush packed in the bowl, and I have enough for three bowl-packs once I cache the first; I even have a half-blunt left over from the impromptu Session yesterday. Physically there is craving; mentally I don't give a flying fuck, and **that** is the dangerous thing. I know what will happen if I blaze up: Chemical Happiness; I know what will happen when I run out: grouch-on-steroids for just over two weeks... followed by slight depression as I adjust to no Delta-9 in the System. Now? Now I simply don't want to **be** High, and don't *care* about the effects on my body and Mind; if my mental Clock didn't flash numbers before my Mind's Eye I'd probably drift into the living room, turn on the Brain Eradicator call television and Dork Out until hunger overwhelmed the caffeine to the point where the nagging itch for a nap stopped dragging my eyelids down.

"Fuck," I exhale. Time to get dressed; I used to enjoy my Layered Look. Now I simply throw on a pair of jogging pants to keep Winter's chill from shredding through the heavy blue jeans like gossamer-thin rice paper; I don't give any serious thought to style. Even when I hit my chest with two sprays of cologne there's no Thought; I jerk on a white short-sleeved tee shirt and snatch up a long-sleeve white shirt to cover that. The only time I actually Think about my style of dress: heavy Winter ski jacket or Duster. Why then? I'm wondering which will catch Assassin Attention first; probably the Duster, as Black Males are not allowed to wear such things in the South **unless** they go for complete Cowboy/Country Style.

I should be worried that the only sensation of Being Alive comes from Thoughts of Life-or-Death Combat, but I am not; these days Death is the **only** Thought capable of making me feel alive. I Feel nothing. The planned trip to the Outside World will only confirm what I already know: I Feel nothing. If I happen to catch a female looking my way I'll smile politely, but I won't **FEEL** any emotion; it will be an instinctive, mechanical reaction... like the cigarillo I've just slipped into my mouth after donning my black rosary. Routine Movements, done so many times I don't think about the action; I look down at the black rosary and try to Feel something of God. Nothing; all I Feel is nothing... and I honestly don't give a shit. That I find this slightly amusing should cause concern, but I cannot dredge up enough *motivation* to be concerned **or** laugh manically at the utter apathy that somehow became Daily Bread and Water.

And strangest of all: my Thoughts about the bowl of Kush resting patiently on my computer desk; if I see a therapist I'll end up drugged silly. According to *science and SOCIETY* I'll be better... **NORMAL**; from what I see around me, **NORMAL** means I'll be another terrified, hypocritical, covetous Bible Thumper eagerly snitching out anyone, **desperate** to feel above everyone... the **only** one worthy of God's Love and attention. *HOWEVER...* if I'm under the influence of marijuana I am a ***THREAT TO SOCIETY'S FABRIC!!!!*** How? Because High I get the Four Symptoms: High, Horny, Munchies, Sleepy; High I am not another money-hungry fuckhead willing to sell my Soul and the Souls of all unborn children for an extra nickel, or to use Normal phraseology: *a productive member of Society.*

Funny thing is: going off my Society-approved meds makes me a ***greater*** threat **TO** Normal Society than purging Delta-9 from my system; even better... the meds don't work unless you visit a therapist. This is, when all is said and done, **paying** someone to listen to you Bitch-and-Moan about shit while having the *sense* of security, the Doctor-Patient bullshit every Assassin and District Attorney learns how to circumvent on Training Day Three; Friends **used** to occupy this niche, but ***TRUST*** is Fine Print in Society today, and guaranteed **ONLY** if you have enough money to buy a lawyer with enough skill to defend it in a Court of Law or influence to get the nudge-nudge-wink-wink brush-over verdict.

Good Weed. While tying my boot laces it dawns on me that I'm actually Thinking Shit Through instead of going on sober instinct; not that instinct has *ever* let me down or been incorrect, mind. High I actually follow the Logic; when I hit a wall or my Thoughts fly off in some random direction I know that the Logic has holes. Have the same thing happen when I'm sober and Anger is my first Reaction... or it *used* to be before Apathy became my normal reaction. Now I simply react, and I don't care about results or consequences; I don't even care **if** I react. If I wasn't breathing I'd be another mindless automaton jerked around by mental programming. High I can smile and whip out a snappy come-back.

Sober... it takes everything I have to curtail my instinctive reaction to the same situation: *they're insulting you... **KILL THEM!!!!*** Sober I view everyone around me as either Friend or Foe, and I **know** their status well before they look my way and eons before they *think* to speak; while High I don't give a shit, and this is a **GOOD THING**. It means I'm willing to let people pleasantly surprise me *instead* of expecting the royal ass-fuck with a venom coated spiked bat: the socially-acceptable Sober Reaction *minus* the socially expected Self-Control. And if I have difficulties with Self-Control go see a doctor and get *LEGAL* drugs and a **PAID** confidant.

Call up ya Boys for a Blunt session and shoot the shit: *UNACCEPTABLE!!!!* Blaze one with your BFF? **NOPE**; this is why we have *alcohol!!!!*

Yeah: Normal Society is perplexing; I save the marijuana for when I return, tamp out the nubbin remnant from the cigarillo and armor-up for my final outing. I pull on a black hooded sweatshirt, hang my rosary over the thick cotton with my left hand has my right hand does a quick pocket check; after I double-check for my keys and wallet I don my black duster. Between the Assassins (they'll get nervous because I don't fit the Standard Black Male Profile and *demand* I produce some form of identification) and the Locals (they'll not-stare at me with Fear plastered behind their carefully controlled facial ticks) I'm sure to find nothing unusual; I'm different, and different is *DEADLY DANGEROUS* here... and in quite a few areas in America these Days and Nights.

And I get glaring proof the instant I step into the bus; I don't know her from a blade of grass, yet judging from the way she cocks back and sneers at my style of dress I do not meet her approval. Of course... the threadbare somewhat black top revealing *the thread count on her pink bra with blue daisies* means **her happy ass** is Top-Shelf Diva; she spares me one last bitchy-glance, catching me slowly pulling my black hood over my forehead and I settle in for the ride, music keeping out bullshit drama-talk and gossip. **THAT** IS NORMAL for any Hood-raised Male; *I just don't DRESS the part!!!!*

Every African American who gets on the bus stares at me as if they've just seen Death; eventually **FEAR** chokes out every other stench. I smile at that; one of the females smells like Gutter-Ho.

If there is something positive, it happens while I'm walking through Wal-Mart; there's a MILF strutting around with her daughters. One is a Carbon Copy... *the other is Gothling*; guess which one smiles politely as I drift by with my meager groceries.

* * * *

I withdrew from everyone I'd met during my six year torture session. I'd been kicked around and pushed for too many months; I'd been abandoned by so-called Friends. Amy chose lingering on my social sites to the occasional word from a close friend; others joined her and eventually I grew to loathe the very **thought** of someone lurking in the electronic ether, treating me like some deep dark Secret. But worse than all of these things, my trip through Corporate Gourmet Fast Food nearly obliterated my Passion for Cooking and the Kitchen; so while I was persona-non-gratis I took time to re-evaluate everything in my existence. I'm not ashamed to say Suicide reared its frightening face here; I've seen it too many times to ignore the blatant Warning its appearance represents.

I'd also stopped tokin' up; for nearly a month straight my body adjusted to the absence of Delta 9 in its internal workings. There's no way to describe the events of that time without stating this: I wasn't a Fiend for a blunt. I'd gone Dry before and knew what to expect; my appetite returned to baseline Three Squares a Day and the liquid fluidity I knew as Thoughts crept to a thick ooze-crawl. In short: I was in the perfect Editor mindset; so I sat in front of my monitor and started gathering the many short stories and scenes together, carefully putting scattered Thoughts into some semblance of Order. What I discovered amazed me: my stories held a decidedly Gothic tone, though many probably consider this *depressing* rather than the emotion-driven Gothic style; yet when written from the perspective of mostly African American Male **suffering** from undiagnosed Clinical Depression the tone not only seemed appropriate, it **resonated** with what I'd experienced both here and back Home in New Orleans.

What surprised me more than anything about being Dry: the *complete* lack of my usual paranoia; don't confuse this with the effect from marijuana use. Between the chemical interaction with normal brain chemistry and the illegal nature of simply obtaining a nickel-bag of Funk, that Paranoia is completely different from what I experience without Delta 9 in the system. **That** Paranoia is my natural tendency to connect disparate events into a fabric which I can better interpret and prepare contingencies for, and it *wasn't* there during my Dry Spell; instead, I found my Thoughts oddly clear. When I searched for a reason I found something I did not expect, though in retrospect... it was something I'd noticed frequently: Fear.

Fear runs The Streets. Bad Guys use Fear to intimidate; law enforcement uses Fear to counteract the Fear Bad Guys use. Mom is afraid of the Nameless Terror outside of the House/Home; Children are taught Fear through mistrust of **anyone** not approved by whoever makes the Rules. Fear is the foundation of Paranoia, and I'd grown fearless during those six years. Several encounters with local idiots with Badges and Guns proved just how fearless I'd become; not only did I find a new fearlessness, I saw within me the disturbing calm many see within fanatics. It was as if the complete lack of Fear allowed extreme apathy to overwhelm my normally paranoid nature. Once that happened I became extraordinarily dangerous; however, instead diving into maddening chaos, I rose up, a thing *incapable of giving a shit!!!*

I remember the day I looked into the bathroom mirror and **tried** to care about my appearance. I remember that day because I couldn't, and *still* went through the motions; there was no passion... no purpose to my actions. Yet apathy didn't bring thoughtlessness to my actions; I simply did what I always did: ensure my Body was Clean. I remember taking clippers to my scruffy beard and smiling grimly when the well-oiled steel sounded like someone choking on large motorized hornets. I smiled because my gaze snapped to certain remaining hairs; they were of one general description: *thick Gray Hairs.*

Six years; within those six years I witnessed more than one person do their damn level best to destroy whatever it was they saw when they looked at me. For six years that thing... that Demon... howled and thrashed in defiance until it had no choice but to leave my flesh to bleed out, exhausted beyond wishing for Death. And when they abandoned it, the thing fell to the ground, blood and flesh desiccating as Time rotted the very bones; yet they did not finish what they started.

I was a Good Soul once; I can be again... **if I choose!!** Amy and the others left pain and suffering heaped upon whispered humiliation; yet these things can only **die** on soil which does not Feed them. And I cannot Care; I cannot dredge up spite or vengeful Thoughts and have neither want or need for Hate. I cannot Feel Love; I cannot Feel regret, mercy, compassion or anything positive. I am beyond Demon now; I am a Man... and I **choose** to *not* allow myself to fester. I choose to be Who and **What** I Am: a Cook and Writer struggling to make an honest living doing not only what I dream, but what I Love and enjoy **despite everyone around me telling me I can't or shouldn't**.

I am fearless. If I choose, I am kind and compassionate. I am cold, ruthless and utterly heartless. I will always be a stalwart Friend and formidable Foe. I am everything and nothing, and this... feels good.

fin

CREDITS

Cover Art: Kenneth Strader
aleoninefashion.wix.com/ksphotography

Back Cover Photograph: Melissa Christina
www.melissachristinaphotography.zenfolio.com

Please check out these talented artists and tell 'em Quick sent
ya!!!